P9-CDA-000

Also by Martine Leavitt

My Book of Life by Angel

Keturah and Lord Death

Heck Superhero

Tom Finder

The Dollmage

The Taker's Key

The Prism Moon

The Dragon's Tapestry

BLUE
MOUNTAIN

MARTINE LEAVITT

MARGARET FERGUSON BOOKS
Farrar Straus Giroux
New York

Farrar Straus Giroux Books for Young Readers
175 Fifth Avenue, New York 10010

Printed in the United States of America by RR Donnelley & Sons Company, Harrisonburg, Virginia
Designed by Roberta Pressel
First edition, 2014
10 9 8 7 6 5 4 3 2 1

mackids.com

Library of Congress Cataloging-in-Publication Data
Leavitt, Martine, 1953–
Blue Mountain / Martine Leavitt. — First edition.
pages cm
Summary: "Tuk, a bighorn sheep of the Canadian Rockies, leads his herd beyond the snares of man and the wiles of predators to the freedom of the blue mountain"—Provided by publisher.
ISBN 978-0-374-37864-6 (hardback)
ISBN 978-0-374-37865-3 (ebook)
1. Bighorn sheep—Juvenile fiction. [1. Bighorn sheep—Fiction. 2. Sheep—Fiction. 3. Survival—Fiction. 4. Endangered species—Fiction. 5. Canadian Rockies (B.C. and Alta.)—Fiction.] I. Title.
PZ10.3.L487Bl 2014
[Fic]—dc23
2014003697

Farrar Straus Giroux Books for Young Readers may be purchased for business or promotional use. For information on bulk purchases please contact Macmillan Corporate and Premium Sales Department at (800) 221-7945 x5442 or by email at specialmarkets@macmillan.com.

For my grandchildren

I do think animals have languages,
but they are entirely truthful languages.
—from "The Question I Get Asked Most Often,"
Wave in the Mind by Ursula K. LeGuin

Love the animals: God has given them
the rudiments of thought and joy untroubled.
—from *The Brothers Karamazov* by Fyodor Dostoyevsky

CONTENTS

BLUE
MOUNTAIN

TUK

Tuk was born in the snow and wind of early spring. He was the biggest lamb born on the lambing cliffs that season, and for seasons out of memory. Gradually, over the generations, bighorns had been getting smaller, but Tuk was a reminder of the herd's former days of greatness.

Soon after his birth Tuk stood on shaky legs. Before the day was out he could run and leap small leaps and keep up with his mother, Pamir, as she grazed on the sparse grasses of the rocky heights.

"Who are we?" he asked Pamir.

"We are the bighorn," she replied. "We live on the mountain's high places, above where most animals can live, above even where the trees can grow."

"Bighorn?" Tuk said. "But your horns are small."

"That is because I am a female," said Pamir. "But you are a male, and when you are grown, a ram, you will have big horns. You will use them only in sport, to prove you are strong enough to father the lambs."

Two other males, Ovis and Rim, were also born on the lambing cliffs that spring, as well as four females: Nai, Mouf, Sto, and Dall.

The nursery band ran and jumped and butted one another playfully. They ran faster each day, zig, zag, darting through the legs of their mothers, and from one end of the meadow to the other. Though Ovis was a good climber, Tuk was at least as good and sometimes could go even higher. They ran races, and though Rim often won, Tuk was almost as fast, and sometimes faster. Nai was graceful and could jump far, but Tuk could jump, too, and sometimes farther. Mouf asked many questions, and Tuk was the one who searched out the answers. Sto was quiet and timid and did not like to venture far from her mother, but sometimes Tuk could persuade her to play.

Dall was calm and steady. She was the one who

decided they had explored a patch of grass enough, and when she sought out a new patch, they all followed. She would only wait for one, and that was Tuk.

After a few days, Pamir said to Tuk, "Tomorrow we return to the main herd. Before we go, I must teach you the most important thing about the bighorn. Listen, and I will tell you an old story."

> When the mountain first created the deer, she said, "Consider my austere beauty. You may have it for your own." The deer said, "The mountain is too rocky and forbidding. We would rather have the lowlands and the brooks, and the woods to hide in, and antlers with which to fight our enemies." And so the mountain gave them their desire.
>
> Then the mountain created the elk and said, "Ponder well my severe beauty. You may have it for your own." The elk said, "We do not want the mountain. It is too steep and cold and craggy. Give us the hills and the valleys and the rushing creeks, and give us bigger antlers even than the deer with which

to fight our enemies." And so the mountain gave them their desire.

When the mountain made Lord Denu, the first of the bighorn, she said to him, "I am rocky and forbidding. I am steep and cold and craggy, but do I not have my own beauty? Will you be the one to have it?"

"Yes," Denu said, "we will, because from the top we can see the lowlands and the brooks and the woods. We can see the hills and the valleys and the rushing creeks. We can see the world."

The mountain was so pleased with Denu's answer that she gave him tricky feet so he could scale the steep places nimbly. She gave him strong jaws and bowels so he could eat the forage that grew out of the mountain. She gave him horns that were thicker and stronger and more powerful than the antlers of the deer and the elk together, but she called Denu the peaceable one.

"Peaceable?" Tuk asked.

"It meant we would survive because of our speed

and agility on the heights, where predators cannot follow," Pamir explained. "We would thrive as a herd at peace with one another, and the bear and the puma and the wolf would see our great numbers and stay away. The mountain cannot be beautiful without us."

SUMMER MEADOW

The next day the nursery band and their mothers left the lambing cliffs to join the main herd at the summer range.

"Now that you are quick and the wind is warm, we go to the sweet grass farther down the mountain," Pamir said to Tuk. "You will meet the yearlings and the barren ewes."

"What are yearlings?" Tuk asked.

"They are the lambs that were born last year."

The lambs and their mothers started down the mountain, past elk-kill meadow and avalanche slope and the lodgepole forest. They passed black stumps in the bracken where the forest had burned long ago, and crossed quick, shallow rivers. The ewes taught their lambs the traditional paths that had been used by the bighorn for countless generations. Tuk, and Rim with him, wanted to explore, but their mothers would not allow it.

"Rams may roam and wander, but ewes and lambs who are wise stay to the ancient trails," Pamir said.

The lambs seemed to have always known the scent of bear scat, and the track of the puma and the call of the wolf. They learned where mineral licks might be found and where the sweetest grasses grew at the edge of the late-melting snow. That evening they bedded down in fleabane and yarrow beside loon lake, and from there Tuk had an unobstructed view of the sky.

Abruptly, the low evening sun broke apart the clouds and he thought he saw the far sky take the shape of a great high mountain, blue and unsolid. Tuk had thought he could see the whole world from the lambing cliffs, but now he saw that the world went on forever.

"Dall, look!" he said, but in the next moment the clouds covered the sun again, and the blue mountain vanished.

"What is it?" Dall asked.

"I thought I saw—" But he had no words to describe a mountain that floated one moment and was gone the next.

The loon called, and Tuk wondered if his life was not only one thing, and not only his. He thought he understood what his mother meant when she taught him that his kind had been always, and he was part of the always.

The next day they walked again, down and down. The rooty trail led them to new delights—beds of gentian and nodding onion, and stretches of soft grass between the stones.

Just before evening a comforting scent came to Tuk—a musky scent like his mother's. Tuk and his nursery band came to a long ridge that overhung a sloping meadow rimmed on the north and south by rock and cliff and pine. The meadow stretched downward in folds and dips and rises, spotted by cloud shadow.

Beyond the meadow the mountain continued westward to drop down in natural terraces of field and forest, finally bottoming out in the hazy distance into a vast valley. Across the valley rose a mountain covered thickly in trees, and beyond that another hazy green mountain, only a little higher than treed mountain. After that was the endless sky.

The mothers led them down from the ridge into the sloping meadow, and as they came the barren ewes and yearlings of the main herd gathered around. There were about twenty of them, and they nosed and nudged the lambs as gently as if they were their own. "Welcome, welcome," they said, "we have been waiting."

After a time everyone fell silent, and the herd parted for an old ewe—old, but not weak or ill. She walked among them as if she had known them since they were lambs, for indeed she had. She was Kenir, the matriarch and leader of the herd.

"Let Kenir see the lambs," some in the herd said.

The mother ewes drew their lambs to their sides and lowered their eyes so none would see their pride.

"Stand tall, Tuk," Pamir said.

Kenir looked solemnly over the new crop of lambs. She sniffed Ovis and Rim and the female lambs and nodded solemnly before Dall.

"This one will be a matriarch someday," she said of Dall.

She looked last at Tuk. Pamir dipped her head to Kenir.

"What is his name?" Kenir asked.

"His name is Tuk."

Kenir looked Tuk over, up and down and around.

"Before man hunted with guns and took our territory, the biggest rams fathered lambs like this one."

The herd murmured. Just at that moment the clouds to the west opened and again Tuk saw the blue mountain.

"What do you see, Tuk?" Kenir asked.

"I thought I saw a mountain made of the sky," he said. "But it is gone now."

"A mountain made of sky?"

"Yes," Tuk said. "It was blue like the sky, and white as a cloud at the top, but it was flat as a dry leaf against the horizon."

The herd made another murmuring sound.

"Have you seen it, then, Tuk?" Kenir said, wondering. "You call it blue mountain, but others have called it story mountain because so few see it, and fewer still believe it is real. The stories say that there the meadows are knee-deep in grass, the streams are never dry, even in summer, and that man never goes there."

"He says he sees story mountain," one ewe whispered to another.

"He calls it blue mountain," said another.

"He is only a lamb."

"But he is a big one," Rim said, defending his friend, "as the lambs were long ago."

Kenir raised her head and gazed over the herd until they were silent. "This Tuk the mountain has given us to keep the herd from dying out," she said. "To him I will tell all my stories."

The herd began to press him. Pamir grunted a warning.

A yearling named Balus said, "How can a lamb, even a big one, keep the herd from dying out? Can he stop man from destroying the winter grazing grounds? Can he stop man and wolf and puma from hunting us?"

Tuk waited for someone to answer, but no one did.

"When I am grown and I have horns, I will fight winter and wolves and man," Tuk said.

The herd laughed. "Perhaps your mother has not taught you that the bighorn are peaceable," an elder ewe said.

"Maybe he is not a bighorn," Balus said. "Maybe he is some other creature."

The yearlings laughed and wandered away to graze, but Tuk's nursery band stayed with him.

"You are too young to save us just yet, Tuk," Pamir said gently. "Go play, all of you."

Kenir and Pamir spoke quietly together, and Tuk bounded away to play with his bandmates. He bolted to the end of the summer meadow, and, reaching its piney borders, he leaped and turned in the air and ran in the other direction. He climbed every protruding rock, and tumbled and chased and played until his sides heaved. Sometimes, Tuk was sure, he could hear the mountain laugh.

EAGLE

One day was like another for Tuk—the warm summer air, an abundance of food, the closeness and comfort of his fellows. At times Tuk would see blue mountain beyond the shadowy green mountains, climbing into the clouds, blue at its roots but white at its peak. Sometimes he would turn away from blue mountain to see Kenir gazing at him, as if disappointed that he was still a lamb, that he was not yet big enough to save them. Then she would call him to her and tell him the stories of their kind.

But Tuk and his mates grew quick and fearless under the watch of the herd. They feasted on every grass, learning the taste of fescue and foxtail, buttercup and betony, twinflower and groundsel. At the height of summer the sun burned the blue out of the sky, the berries weighed down their branches in the heat, the grasses baked, and the warblers slept in the shade.

Eventually the lambs were too big to nurse anymore. "Now you must get all of your strength from the food the mountain grows," Pamir said to Tuk, pushing him away. No longer would she be his mother. Kenir and the other barren ewes would watch over the lambs now.

Sto was grazing unhappily a distance from her mother when Balus saw her and said, teasing, "Sto, I see you are scared to be so far from your mother. You had better run back."

Tuk put himself between her and Balus. "Don't be afraid, Sto," Tuk said. "We are the bighorn, the lords of the mountain. Watch!" He lowered his head and said to the grass, "Feed me!" He plucked a mouthful of grass sweetly with his teeth. Rim laughed.

"Lords of the mountain?" Balus said to his mates standing nearby. "If we are lords of the mountain, why does man hunt us at his will? Why does the herd shrink year by year until it offers no safety?"

Tuk put his nose to the golden cinquefoil that quivered in the breeze at his feet. "I command you to shine," he said to the flower, and so it did, like a tiny yellow sun in the grass.

All Tuk's bandmates laughed, but Balus scowled.

"Spin!" said Tuk to a spider that spun its web in a bush.

"You must do as he says," said Dall, and they both looked on proudly as the spider continued to spin.

"Lie still," Rim said to a rock.

"Sing," said Ovis to the nuthatch in the tree.

"Blow," said Dall to the wind.

"You see, Sto?" Tuk said. "All is as we would wish it to be."

Sto looked up. "Fly!" she called in her timid voice. The others looked and saw a golden eagle hovering on the hard sky with wings like pine boughs. "Fly and dive!"

As if it had heard, the eagle banked and dipped and down, down it swooped.

"Run!" Tuk cried.

The lambs scattered, all but Sto, who gazed up, enthralled. Tuk ran back toward her. "Sto! Come!"

The eagle fell from the sky, but Sto did not move. Tuk saw the eagle's sharp wings and its blade of a beak and saw it pounce into the meadow and rise again with a lamb in its talons.

Tuk saw that it was Sto.

She was lifted up and up and her white coat got smaller until she was a star in the day sky, until the eagle, flying toward blue mountain, vanished.

Tuk heard no sound. Sto did not bleat, the eagle did not cry. It might not have been, except that Sto was gone from the herd. The meadow was quiet. Tuk was surprised most of all by the silence inside him.

He felt as if the meadow had shifted under his feet. His bandmates gathered together closely, but Tuk stood apart, staring in the direction the eagle had flown, in the direction of blue mountain that might only be a story.

"Lord of the mountain, how will you save the herd?" Balus said close behind Tuk. "You couldn't even save a lamb from a bird."

He went away, but his words rattled in Tuk's head.

Kenir approached the nursery band. Tuk still

gazed in the direction the eagle had flown. When Kenir came close, he said, "The eagle took Sto because I did not fight him."

"No," Kenir said. "Because our numbers have dwindled, we have little protection from predators who would stay away if we were a large, healthy herd."

"Why? Why have our numbers dwindled?"

"Winter," she said.

"I am not afraid of winter."

"Are you not?" Kenir said. "In winter, snow covers the mountain, the ground, the grass. Squirrels sleep in holes in the trees, marmots keep warm underground, the puma has her cave, and wolves their lairs. But the bighorn has nothing but the mountain. The bighorn does not sleep through the winter like the bear. In winter we are hungry."

Tuk did not know hunger, and anyway he could not think what it had to do with eagles and Sto and sorrow like a thistle in his throat.

"In winter," Kenir continued, "we leave the summer meadow and go down out of the mountain to the winter valley where the snow is not so deep. And what do you think we find there, Tuk?"

"Grass," said Tuk.

"Yes. We should find grass under the snow, waiting for us—grass that has grown all summer long undisturbed. But men come with their tame sheep and graze the grass to stubble, and we catch their diseases against which we have no resistance. Now man has built a wide trail between the mountain and our winter feeding grounds, and on it many of our number are killed by man's machines. Last year, they began to build dwellings in the valley, filled with the light of the sun even at night. We come back to the mountain fewer than we left, and as our numbers lessen, our predators grow fatter—the puma, the wolf, the eagle."

She waited a time for him to speak, and when he did not, she turned away, saying, "Today, Tuk, you are older. Do not blame yourself."

FALL RAMS

The grass began to brown and grow dry as summer moved into fall. Every day the lambs played, but not as they had before the eagle. The sun came up each morning later and smaller than the day before. The meadow of a morning was white with frost, and though the slanting light burned off the frost by mid-day, it returned again in the evening. Each day the frost pinched Tuk's ears and hooves harder. Often he would gaze in the direction of blue mountain, as if he thought the eagle would bring Sto back.

One morning a ram stepped princely into the meadow, sporting a great crown of horn. He stood still, wary and proud, his nostrils quivering. All the herd lifted their heads to acknowledge him.

Kenir approached the lambs and said, "He is here for the rut, the mating time. His name is Churo, and once he was my lamb."

The ram bent his head to graze. The great muscles in his shoulders moved like a river of water under his sleek coat.

A short time later two more rams emerged from the border of trees onto the ridge, and over time four more, each with three-quarter-curl horns. The rams drew together, when they were not grazing, and wrestled with one another.

"For now it is spirited and playful jostling," Kenir explained to the band. "But the rams are also testing one another's strength. In play they are establishing rank."

"You mean soon they will fight?" Tuk said.

"They will battle, yes," Kenir said. "Not to kill or to maim—only to establish which of them will father most of the lambs. When the rut is over, the rams will resume their friendship and travel together again in small bands."

Tuk and Rim and Ovis shoved and jostled one another playfully as the rams did.

At last came not a prince but a king of rams. He

was alpha and old, with full-curl horns. The moment he stepped into the meadow, the other rams stepped away.

"He is Dos," Kenir said. "The king." Behind him came another ram, almost as large as Dos, and just as beautiful. "That is his friend, Tragus."

The rams became more active and aggressive as the moon fattened. Each morning they huddled. The smaller rams nibbled at the horns of the larger ones, rubbed their faces, and were permitted liberties. Sometimes, for no reason, a ram would suddenly whirl about and bound downhill. Another would follow, and a mock battle would ensue.

The battle began in earnest, however, when Dos walked regally down into the meadow to claim Sham as his ewe. Tragus challenged him.

"You are old, Dos, my friend," Tragus said. "A year older than I." He spoke as if it were a game or a sport. "Surely you are too tired to fight for ewes anymore."

"Let's see!" Dos said, and he lowered his horns.

Tragus rose up in a threat stance and charged.

Clash!

The sound of horn on horn rang across the meadow and echoed off the cliff face. Tuk thought it was the most magnificent sound he had ever heard—greater than the sound of a tree falling, or a waterfall, or thunder.

Threat stance, clash!

Threat stance, clash!

Tragus reeled away.

"Next year, Tragus," Dos said, panting.

But after a short rest, Tragus rose up on his hind legs and again charged.

Clash!

Clash!

Clash!

The sounds burst against Tuk's ears like great boulders falling from the heights to the rocks below.

For hours Dos and Tragus fought. All day and half into the evening Tuk watched.

At last, when the whole sky was filled with fierce color and the meadow glowed gold, Tragus turned away and Dos claimed Sham as his ewe.

"Someday we will be rams and fight," Tuk said to Rim and Ovis, and they looked at one another with pride.

"Yes," said Balus behind them. "And I will beat you."

THE PUMA CHILD

That evening, just as the herd was bedding down, came the cry: "Puma!"

"Climb! Climb the cliffs!" called the rams.

As though he had heard it many times before, Tuk knew the sound of the puma's soft step into the meadow.

"Climb!" called the ewes and the yearlings.

"Climb! Climb!"

Alongside Rim, Tuk ran to the cliff, but he slowed when he heard Mouf's cry behind him. He would not allow the puma to have his bandmate Mouf as he had allowed the eagle to have Sto.

"Go ahead of me, Mouf," Tuk said. "Climb fast!"

She leaped ahead onto a ledge of the cliff face.

"Keep climbing!" he called. "I'm right here."

Tuk heard a snarl and turned to see the puma and her child not far behind him. The kitten had faint spots and was not much bigger than himself, but the puma, softly golden as sunbaked grass, looked as heavy as a ram.

He could climb no higher because Mouf had stopped and was blocking his way.

"Climb higher, Mouf! Their footing isn't as good as ours. As we go higher, the ledges get narrower and they will stop following us."

Behind him, Tuk heard the puma say to her child, "Hunt."

The puma child sprang up onto the outcropping below Tuk.

"The mountain is mine, too," he said, baring his teeth.

"Jump higher," Tuk said to Mouf. She jumped up and Tuk took her place on the cliff face.

The puma child followed, leaping to the ledge Tuk had just left. He swatted at Tuk's hind leg.

"Again, Mouf," Tuk said.

She leaped again to a ledge a little higher. Tuk stayed between her and the young cat. Still the puma child followed, leap for leap. The cliff face became steeper. The rock wall was in Tuk's left eye, and the black sky and the moon in his right eye.

Tuk wished he had been born with teeth for breaking bones. He wished his small budding horns were bigger. But all he had was his agility on the mountain. Above, he could see the herd reaching the top of the cliff one by one, gathering together on the ridge. Again the young cat swiped at him and snarled.

"Mouf," Tuk said, "if you don't move, I am puma food."

She looked back for the first time and saw the puma child close. Her eyes rolled in fear and she leaped—to a wider, lower ledge.

"Not lower!" Tuk said. "Higher!" He could see the young cat studying his advantage. He was no longer looking at Tuk at all—his eyes were wide as a mouth.

Tuk leaped to a higher ledge. "Mouf, you must get higher than the puma child."

"I'm almost as high as the moon, Tuk," she said.

The puma child crouched to pounce on her.

"Mouf, do what I say." Tuk saw the muscles

ripple under the young cat's fur. He lowered his voice. "I will jump down to your spot, and you jump up to mine—at the same time. Switch!"

He jumped down. Mouf jumped up—just as the puma child leaped to where she had been.

Tuk and the puma child were together on the ledge. Tuk scooted backward, away from the cat's sharp teeth, as far as he could go. His hind feet were on the vanishing edge of the shelf. The puma was a good climber, but not as good as a bighorn, and he did not have firm footing. He batted a thick paw at Tuk's face.

"Kill," hissed the puma mother below.

"I will fight you," Tuk said.

"Bighorn don't fight." Again the puma child swatted at Tuk with his heavy paw.

Tuk thought of the eagle. "I fight," he said.

He butted the puma child with his lamb horns. He butted as if the puma child were the eagle, as if he were Balus saying *I will beat you*, as if he were man and wolf and winter. He butted the puma child hard.

The puma child scrabbled at the rock with his claws, scrabbled for foothold on the ledge, and fell.

He fell

and fell

into the deep well of the dark

and landed with a thud onto the black below.

Tuk's left side was pressed against the stone wall. The rest of him was in air, trembling. Slowly he moved his back feet onto the thickest part of the ledge. He saw the mother puma below, sniffing at her dead child. She looked up at Tuk, her green eyes turned white, reflecting the moon.

"You killed my kitten," she said. Her voice was measured and purrful. "I will specialize. I will raise my next kitten on this herd, and the next kitten, and the next. I will hunt your herd, and especially you . . . Tuk." She opened her mouth wide to show all her teeth and slunk away into the dark.

"The puma knows your name," Mouf said quietly.

Bighorn never felt dizzy, but Tuk was dizzy now, looking down at the puma child broken on the rocks below. He could not be sorry that it was the puma child and not him, that it was the puma child dead in the dark and not Mouf. But he remembered what Balus had said, that maybe he was not a bighorn, that maybe he was some other kind of creature.

More slowly now, and with much urging and assuring, he helped Mouf reach the top of the cliff. Once they were onto the ridge, Mouf and Dall and Tuk's other bandmates pressed him and licked his face, nudging closely.

"Is Tuk saving us now?" asked a ewe.

"Only Mouf, and she is so small she hardly counts," said another.

"He pushed the puma child," Balus said. "I saw."

The herd looked at Tuk in silence, waiting for him to deny it, but Tuk said nothing. One ewe sniffed him. "He *smells* like a bighorn," she said.

Gradually the herd made their way slowly back to the meadow.

"Come, Tuk," Mouf said. But he did not come.

"Come, Tuk," Rim said.

But he would not come, even when Dall led his bandmates back to the safety of the herd.

Tuk stayed alone at the top of the cliff in the dark, and the puma child stayed still at the bottom of the cliff, and if the white light of the moon touched them both, neither of them knew it.

NOT TODAY

In the morning Tuk awoke on the ridge. He opened his eyes only a little, without moving, and then closed them again quickly.

Dos, the king ram, and Kenir were standing beside him.

"Kenir, I have traveled to the south of this mountain, but there the mountains are all trees and no meadow. I have traveled to the east, but there the mountains are all rock and no meadow. This past summer I traveled to the north, but there the mountains gradually flatten into territory that is good for elk and deer, but not for bighorn. All that is left is the west, and that way is closed in with thickly treed mountains."

"This one says he has seen a mountain to the west," Kenir said. "He calls it blue mountain." Tuk felt they were both looking at him now.

"Story mountain?" Dos said. "All my life they said it was like the fog we wade in at daybreak, like the clouds that vanish with the sun. It was not made of stone and earth like this mountain, they said. It was a dream, a wish, or a tale you tell in a storm to keep you warm."

Tuk could not pretend to be sleeping any longer. He stood up, and said, "I have seen it!"

Dos fixed his golden eye on Tuk.

"Tuk," Kenir said. Tuk remembered his manners and performed a low-stretch bow to Dos.

"You're big," Tuk said to Dos.

"Big enough to eat a lamb in a bite or two," Dos said.

"I'm big for a lamb," Tuk said.

"Three bites, then," Dos answered.

"Our kind doesn't eat flesh," Tuk said.

"So that's what was causing my indigestion."

"I have seen blue mountain, sir. Can you lead us there?"

"It is the matriarch who leads the herd, west or otherwise," Dos said.

"But it is for rams to explore," Kenir replied.

After a pause, Dos said respectfully to Kenir, "I would speak with this Tuk alone."

Kenir nodded and walked away.

When they were alone Dos asked kindly, "Is it true you pushed the puma child?"

Tuk was high enough to see the whole herd below, his bandmates and Balus and the yearlings looking up in wonder to see him talking to Dos. Tuk was high enough to see the barren ewes that had been like mothers to him, and the proud rams. He was high enough to see how the bighorn lived gently on the mountain, graceful on the steeps, strong on the tough alpine grasses, and how they found safety in fellowship.

He looked down at the puma child far below on the rocks. "Yes," he said. "I fought."

Tuk wondered if Dos had heard him, because for a time he did not speak.

"Someday, Tuk," he said at last, "you will have big horns. With them you could fight a lone wolf, but wolves are seldom alone. My horns cannot protect me from a hunting pack. Even if they could, I cannot protect every weak or sick or aged bighorn in the herd, or every lamb. My horns do not protect me from man, from their hunger for our territory or from their guns. But the mountain gave us gifts—feet to climb the steeps and teeth to find forage on the heights, and strong bodies and thick coats so we need not fear the cold, and noses that can read the wind, and, most of all, our stories that we pass down through the generations so no trail is lost, no lesson unlearned. As a herd, we are strong."

Tuk lowered his eyes. "When I did not save Sto from the eagle, I wished to save Mouf from the puma."

"Ah. Yes, I heard of the eagle. I was very sorry."

"Maybe I am not the usual kind of bighorn."

Dos looked down to the rocks below. "You stayed here all night to be alone, to be ashamed. Are you done being alone and ashamed?"

Tuk could not answer that question, so instead he said, "Let's tell Kenir that we should go to blue mountain today!"

Dos stared west, and then he laughed and shook

his head. "Not today, Tuk. Today the sun shines. Today the ewes want courting, and I am the king. But perhaps tomorrow—"

Bang!

The air cracked with a noise like rock on rock.

Dos leaped one way. Tuk leaped another, the taste of metal in his mouth.

Bang!

Below, the rams and the whole herd scattered and ran.

The ringing sound of gunshot filled Tuk's mouth and echoed off the cliffs. He sought the safety of the cliff and stayed there a long time, perched above the body of the puma child.

EARLY SNOW

Men came to the meadow, but Dos and the other rams had run to where they could not find them. The men tromped about and called, but eventually they left and Tuk lost the sight and the scent of them.

The sunlight was slantwise when Tuk and his mates returned to the meadow. Kenir and Pamir and a few old ewes had already wandered back and were grazing as if everything were usual. The wind had picked up by the time the rams also began to creep back from where they had fled.

At twilight Dos limped into the meadow. His right foreleg was black with blood. Kenir hung her head and stopped grazing. The great ram stood tall on three feet and held the other off the ground, quivering. After a time he lay painfully down, and Tuk went to stand beside him. Dos seemed not to see that Tuk was near, and Tuk remained silent and still.

A short time later the wind began to blow hard and cold. The herd and Tuk's bandmates walked around Dos and away, heading toward a bit of shelter amid the rocks. Tragus came last and stood silently beside Dos for a long time without speaking. Finally he gave Dos a low-stretch bow and walked slowly away.

Soon snow was falling fiercely, blowing over Dos and through Tuk's legs, and Tuk saw that Dos would not be able to stand up and paw away the snow to get his food. He would starve.

As the snow began to accumulate, Kenir called for Tuk to come. When he did not, she came and bowed before Dos. "Tell Tuk to go to shelter," she said.

Dos looked at Tuk as if he had not known he was there all along. "Go, Tuk, before you are trapped by drifting snow," he said. His voice had lost its power.

"If you go, I will go," Tuk said.

Kenir stamped her foot. "Dos is waiting for Lord Denu." When Tuk said nothing she nodded to something behind him. "Come for his sake, then." Tuk turned and saw Rim waiting a few steps behind him. "He won't come until you do."

"Go, Tuk," Dos said, and this time his voice was commanding. "It is not the way of our kind to disrespect the elder."

"Come with me," Tuk said.

Dos looked away, in the direction of blue mountain.

"I am for the puma," he said softly. "After she finds me, she won't be hungry again for a long time. You must find a way west from the winter valley to blue mountain before she hunts again." The old king held his horns high to the wind. "Son, it is the only way to save the herd."

Tuk thought about that word *son* for a time. It could be true that the son of a king could do such a thing, could find a way to blue mountain.

The wind blew snow into Dos's face and eyes, but he lay still as stone, still as the mountain, and as silent. The high grasses around him bent and bowed before the wind, and then lay quietly under the snow.

Tuk knew Dos would not speak to him anymore. "I'm ready, Rim," he said softly to his friend. Together they trudged through the snow toward the shelter.

At the shelter, a place where two rock walls formed a wedge, the bandmates pressed close to one another. Still they suffered from the cold.

In the dark, Tuk thought he saw, in his half dreaming, the puma child's eyes, hungry and afraid, just before he fell. In the place where Tuk's horns had begun to grow, where they itched and were tender, he felt the warmth and softness of the young cat's fur when he pushed. In one horn he was glad, but in the other he was sad. Half of him belonged in the herd, among the peaceable, and half of him was a strange creature who did not belong. He wondered what a man would feel like against his horns.

At some point in the night, the snow stopped. Tuk awoke, listening. He looked into the dark for Dos, but the old ram had not come. Again he dozed, but even in his sleep he was aware of the cold. He woke early when the wind began to blow again, but now it was a warm wind, and the snow was melting.

"A Chinook," Kenir said. "The mountain sends the warm wind in tribute to a king."

When light came, the herd slowly walked to where they had left Dos. Puma tracks surrounded the body of the old king, and the herd wandered away—all in silence.

The rest of the day the lambs were solemn with their first snow. They did not speak of Dos. They knew something of the mountain they hadn't known before, and something of themselves.

"I am sad," Mouf said.

"We are all sad," Nai said.

"But I am the most sad," Mouf said.

The rams walked away from the herd in small groups, not to return to the main herd until the next fall. Tragus left last of all. On the ridge he looked back, as if he were saying goodbye. Tuk saw that he did not look in the direction of the ewes, but in the direction of Dos's body. Then he turned and vanished over the ridge.

Tuk looked for the sharp-edged clouds in the west to vanish and for blue mountain to appear, but it did not.

WINTER VALLEY

The next day, in the herdish way of the bighorn, they decided almost as one to begin their journey to the winter valley. Kenir went first.

Winter had turned the world white and hard as horn. Snow covered the brittle grasses needed for food to keep them warm. Kenir showed Tuk and his bandmates where to find frozen leaves and berries still on the bushes that the bears had not eaten. She taught the lambs how to paw away the snow to find the crushed and frosty grasses beneath. But mostly they were hungry and cold.

"How long does winter last?" Mouf asked.

"As long as we can bear it," Dall said.

"How long can I bear it?"

“As long as winter lasts.”

The trail first bordered ice-encrusted shale, then wound through a stand of pines and down a steep rocky face. They walked and walked, but at the end of the day, they were still in winter.

“Tomorrow morning we will come in sight of the winter valley,” Kenir promised.

They scraped their beds and lay close to one another in the snow. Tuk could feel Dall trembling next to him. She put her cold nose against him, and he tried his best to be warm for her. He realized her trembling came as much from being in an unfamiliar place as it did from the cold, even though the trail had been used by generations of bighorn.

He fell asleep with Dos’s words in his ears: *Find a way west to blue mountain. It is the only way to save the herd.*

They arose when it was still dark. Tuk’s dreams vanished like the small clouds of his breath as he rose stiff-legged and starving. He searched for tasteless grass beneath the snow until Kenir said it was time for them to go.

They walked in the dark, and all along the way

they found nothing but snow for drinking and leafless twigs when they were forced to walk through trees.

"I want to go back," Mouf said.

"Stop complaining," said Nai.

"When you have no food in your belly, chewing on a complaint or two can bring a little comfort," Dall said kindly.

"Then I shall complain of having to listen to Mouf's whining," Nai replied.

"That is not peaceable," Mouf said.

"Neither is complaining."

"I will think about that," Mouf said.

"Please hurry," Nai said.

"Hush, we are almost there," said Kenir. "Just past that stone outcropping we shall come to a ridge that overlooks the valley."

Tuk's band ran ahead of the others, out onto the lip of the ridge. Tuk stopped, his toes at the very edge of the rock ledge, nothing but air beneath his nose. The newly risen sun was paling the clouds to the west.

All the herd, one by one, perched themselves in a row on the rock ledge, wondering, until finally

Kenir came. The old matriarch took one look and stood rigid, her nostrils quivering.

Below them, stretching west, was a vast valley, but even though Kenir had described it to him, it was not as Tuk imagined.

At the bottom of the last steep fall was a wide human trail, black, with a line running down the middle of it. It stretched from horizon to horizon, and along it man machines raced as quick as an eagle could fly. They roared as they approached and whined as they passed. Beyond that, human dwellings dotted the valley like enormous beaver dams. Great lifeless monster machines with toothen metal scoops lay still beside giant beds of dug earth, heaped into hills and covering the forage. Only a small pasture of grass remained at the foot of treed mountain on the west side of the valley.

"Man has completely despoiled the valley," Kenir said.

After a long silence, an elder ewe said, "What will we do, Kenir?"

Kenir's words bit sharper than the wind. "We will starve if we don't go. We must live in the corner man does not want."

"Maybe he wants all of it," Mouf said. "Maybe it is time for Tuk to save us."

The herd turned their eyes to Tuk.

When he understood they were waiting for him to speak, he said, "We know man only hunts the rams. And maybe the predators will stay away because we are so close to man."

Balus snorted, but Kenir nodded. "We have no choice." She began to tread her way down the steep and toward the road.

Dall followed, and then the rest of the herd. Tuk came last.

No one knew what Dos had told him to do in the snowstorm that night. No one knew but him.

The man trail was like nothing Tuk had seen on the mountain—not stone, not earth, not wood. It smelled like man, like guns, like burnt stumps. It smelled of old blood.

"Many animals have died on this trail," Kenir said. "Man machines run along it and destroy any in its path."

Suddenly she ran across the black trail, and most of the herd ran behind her, including Tuk and his band. The trail clicked under his feet. On the other side, he slowed and turned.

Balus and two of his mates were standing on the road, licking it.

"Balus, come!" Tuk called.

"I'm not afraid," he answered.

"He's licking the salt," Kenir said. "In this way the man machines trick you."

Just then a machine roared up the black trail. Tuk closed his eyes, waiting for some sound of death. But it did not come.

He opened his eyes. The machine had stopped, growling, and Balus was safe. With a baleful look at the machine, Balus and his mates slowly moved across the trail, and the machine raced away.

The whole herd stood in awe of Balus, even Tuk, for whom Balus reserved a pointed smile.

Tuk had seen Kenir wary and alert, but he had never seen her afraid as she was now, leading the herd into the valley. The monster machines were silent and motionless beside the great pits and piles of earth. Farther off was the tumble of human dwellings, full of the rich and overpowering scent of man, sweet as lilies, bitter as poison plants.

Kenir led them as far from the machines as she could to a place where the snow was undisturbed. There they found grass beneath the thin snow, but it was meager, as if it had already been grazed down.

When the sun was fully risen, a man climbed inside one of the monster machines. With a crack and a roar like a mountain storm, the machine came to life. The machine showed no interest in the herd, though it moved and growled. It only wanted to eat the earth.

"The monsters seem to mean no harm to us," Tuk said, but the herd clumped together in fear. Tuk wandered away, walking slowly along the edge of treed mountain, grazing on wolf willow.

"Tuk," Kenir called. "Stay with us."

"I am looking for a trail west," he said, "to blue mountain."

Balus snorted. "Blue mountain. Story mountain, you mean."

His yearling mates snickered.

"We know of no trail, Tuk," Pamir said. "You see that thick forests guard the way, and everywhere treed mountain is flanked by his brother mountains, all of them pathless."

"Bighorn need sight lines," said an elder ewe.

"Bighorn need rocks to climb," said another.

"Bighorn do not migrate," Balus said. "But then, perhaps Tuk is not a bighorn."

WOLVES

In the winter valley it was always more night than day, the clouds bore snow instead of rain, and the sun shone cold. So the winter passed. During the coldest times, the man machines stood quiet, not hungry for the frozen ground. Every day Tuk, sometimes with Rim or Ovis beside him, foraged the west perimeter of the valley, looking for a breach in the forest that might lead over treed mountain. But the lowermost branches of the pines seemed to root themselves into the ground, and the dense overgrowth forbade entrance. If there was a trail, the trees guarded the secret well.

After many days the herd had grazed every inch

of the snow-bleached grass, and even the brush and willow at the forest's edge was depleted.

"I have a pain," Mouf said one evening.

"A pain?" Tuk asked.

"Yes. In my middle."

Rim walked all around Mouf, studying her middle from various angles.

"No, you don't," he said.

"It isn't on my outside. It's on my inside," Mouf said.

Tuk and Dall looked at each other. Starvation found the smallest first.

"Am I dying?" she asked.

"No. You're just hungry," Tuk said.

"How long do you have to be hungry before you are dying?" Mouf asked.

"I don't know," Tuk said, "but we will all find out together."

Just then, Tuk raised his nose. A breeze in the brambles. The machines, the garbage heaps of man, the pines, and—

There!

Wolf!

Not one. Two. And close.

"Wolf!" he said to his bandmates.

At first he could not tell from which direction the wolves were coming. The cross breezes and the man smells confused him. His haunches quivered, his lungs burned with frozen air.

He smelled them again, stronger this time.

"Wolf!" he called again, so the herd could hear.

Others took up the cry.

Every muscle drove him to climb to safety, but there were no rocks to climb in the valley.

The band leaped and scattered in alarm. The wolves, wherever they were, were unconcerned now with stealth. They did not fear man as much as the puma did. They were coming, and quickly.

Where to go? Where to go? Nowhere! The valley was flat and unbroken, except for the man dwellings and—and their monster machines like small hills—

"Follow me!" Tuk said to Dall, and as she did, so did the others. Running, he led his bandmates, and behind them the rest of the herd, across the flat—straight toward the herd of monster machines.

"Where are you going?" Dall gasped for air at his flank.

"Come! Come!" Tuk called.

The wolves were behind—he could hear their footpads, their panting.

Nai's and Mouf's eyes were rolling with fear.

Tuk ran toward the machines, closer, closer, until he felt squeezed by fear before him and behind.

"Jump!" he cried. "Climb up!" In a single bound, fleet and nimble, Tuk leaped onto one of the machines as if it were a pile of stones.

In a moment all his bandmates were perched beside him, and a breath or two later the rest of the herd also leaped gracefully onto the machines. Huddling close together, they had just enough room.

The two wolves paced on the ground below, their tongues dripping. Their feet were not made for clinging to small, slippery places. They could not climb.

Tuk could not get the fight out of his mouth.

"Go away, dogs," he said.

One wolf, a female as gray as the moon behind a cloud, gazed up at him.

"Do you call us dogs?"

"I do," said Tuk.

"Hush," Dall said.

The white wolf lifted his nose at Tuk as if

memorizing his scent. The gray wolf snarled and leaped at the machine, trying to get some footing. In the next moment the wolves spooked at some movement near the man's dwelling and ran to the moon shadow behind the machines.

"Am I really standing on this man thing?" Ovis whispered.

"We might be dreaming," said Mouf.

Just then Tuk saw a lone bighorn. It was Sham, and she was running, running toward them. The wolves, prowling on the other side of the monster machines, looking for a way up, had not seen her yet.

"Make room!" Tuk said.

"There is no room!" Balus called from another machine.

Sham ran toward them, and now the wolves caught her scent.

"Help!" Sham cried as the wolves ran around the machine and saw her.

"Here!" Tuk called. "There's room for you here. Now, Sham, switch!"

Tuk jumped down as Sham jumped up.

And before Tuk, face-to-face, the wolves.

Tuk leaped.

In a single liquid bound he leaped over their heads and ran. Speed, agility, trickery—he ran across the valley floor, straight toward the human dwellings. Fast, fast, faster he ran, shattering the clouds of his own breath before him.

The wolves were close behind him, running steady and untiring. They would follow until he slowed from exhaustion, and Tuk knew, at this speed, that would be soon.

"This is the young one that called us dogs," panted gray wolf behind him.

"For that we shall gnaw on him before he is dead," said white wolf.

Without slowing, Tuk saw, at the edge of his vision, the gray wolf's moon-shadow lift into the air and soar toward the shadow of his own haunches.

Bang!

Gunshot shook the shadows.

Tuk leaped and saw gray wolf spinning in the air. As Tuk landed on his feet, gray wolf landed dead on the ground.

White wolf dashed back toward treed mountain and slipped into the dense forest—vanished as if he had never been.

How had he slid in so easily?

Tuk could hear the stillness of the gray wolf, no movement of blood or breath. He turned away from the man dwellings and loped toward the monster machines. Once, he stopped and glanced back to the place where white wolf had entered treed mountain.

Tuk's bandmates jumped down as he approached.

"Why aren't there wolf bites out of you?" Mouf asked.

"Man shot the gray wolf," Tuk said, panting. "The white wolf disappeared into treed mountain." Dall sniffed at him to be sure he wasn't injured.

Slowly, cautiously, one by one, the rest of the herd jumped off the machines and stood opposite Tuk.

"You jumped right over them, Tuk," Sham said.

"What made you think of climbing the machines, Tuk?" Kenir asked. "How did you know it would be safe?"

"I saw they only roared and moved when man rode them," he said.

The herd, including his bandmates, stared at him.

"What kind of animal are you?" Balus said quietly.

"The wolves smelled our weakness, our sickness," Tuk said. "It is just as you said to me, Kenir. The herd is dying. White wolf will come again, and he may bring others. Next time he will know what to do differently. And even if he doesn't come, the puma waits for us in the summer meadow. Man will build more of their dwellings. Now is the time to go to blue mountain. We must try."

Tuk found that one who had been chased by wolves was not as afraid to go on a long journey to a new place as he might have been before.

"Things are bad here, but we do not know if they will be worse over the mountain," Balus said. "In any case, you have searched all winter and found no trails fit for bighorn."

"I may have found a way," Tuk said. "I saw the white wolf vanish into the mountain, as if there were a breach. If he could go in, maybe a bighorn . . ."

"Ah. He will take us where the wolf has gone. How good," said Balus.

"But I—"

"I, I, I. You sound like a jay," said Balus. "The

bighorn do not speak this way. We are the herd. If we go, we go as *we*, together. It seems *we* have all agreed to stay."

"No," Dall said. She stepped to Tuk's side, facing the rest of the herd. "If it is true that Tuk has found a breach into treed mountain, we—he and I—will go. Any of you are welcome to come with us."

Rim went to Tuk's side, and then Ovis and Nai and Mouf.

The herd, even the yearlings, were silent for a moment, chewing on Dall's words.

Finally Kenir spoke.

"Winter is all but over, Dall. The lambs will come soon. Think about them—the mother ewes need cliffs on which to bear their lambs. If the lambs were born on the trail . . . Well, it is bad here, but at least back on our mountain the lambs will have a chance."

Dall nodded. "Then we have two matriarchs now," she said.

ELK AND TREED MOUNTAIN

The next day, when both the sun and the moon were in the sky, Dall and Tuk and the rest of their bandmates walked together toward the place where he had seen the wolf disappear into the mountain forest. The rest of the herd followed, curious.

Tuk stopped when he saw wolf tracks. The smell of wolf lingered, but he could see no breach. He peered into the forest where the wolf prints vanished.

"How could he go far into underbrush this dense?" Rim asked.

Just then Tuk saw that a solitary elk was watching them from a short distance.

Tuk dipped his head respectfully. "Elk, your

kind travels in the dense woods. Tell us—is there a breach here for us to be able to enter the forest of treed mountain?"

The elk turned her head to look away. "I am beautiful," she said.

"Yes, you are beautiful," Tuk said. "But we are looking for a pathway up treed mountain. Do you know a way?"

She seemed surprised.

"Why would I speak to you at all, given that I am so beautiful? Elk do not concern ourselves with questions."

"Dall and Nai and Mouf are beautiful, too," Tuk said.

"No. Only me," the elk said. "Only the beautiful animals should live. That marmot, for example, is not beautiful." And she turned away.

Tuk and the others looked down to see a marmot at their feet.

"Marmot, how did the wolf get into the mountain? Is there a path nearby?"

"No," he said. "No path." He gripped a stem of snowy oat grass in both paws. "But since you are not the elk, and since you do not eat marmot, and since you are so polite, I have an inclination to tell you that just past these first few trees is a dry creek bed."

"A dry creek bed?"

"You could climb to the clearing at the top of the mountain by this creek bed," the marmot said. "But you must go quickly. The snow is beginning to melt, and when it does, the creek fills with rushing melt-water."

"Will you show us?" Tuk asked.

The marmot chewed on the grass thoughtfully, then nodded his head and disappeared into a fold in the underbrush. Dall ducked low and followed and Tuk and Rim came right behind.

In a moment the green gloom opened to reveal a rocky avenue that climbed up the mountain, wide enough for a grown bighorn. The trees made a canopy overhead, but as high as Tuk could see, the riverbed climbed.

It went against Tuk's every instinct to be in the wood, without long sight lines to allow him to run from predators. "Can we do it?" he asked.

"I can do it," Dall said. "Can you?"

"I'll show you," Tuk said.

"I'll show you, too," Rim said.

"You both will," Dall answered.

They emerged from the forest into the open and told their bandmates about the creek bed. The main herd, bunched together a little way off, murmured.

"It is time to go," Dall said.

"Yes," said Mouf. "Someday. When I am ready."

"Now," Dall said softly.

"Now," Mouf said. "Now is when I will be ready."

Tuk turned to the herd. "I will come back for you," he said. "When we have found blue mountain, I will come back and show you the way."

Sham stepped out of the herd. "May I come with you?" she asked.

Sham was mild-spoken and always stayed in the middle of the herd, so everyone was surprised.

"But you have a lamb in you," Kenir said.

"That is why I must," Sham said.

"Aren't you afraid of places without trails?"

"Yes," Sham said. "But I love Wen more than being afraid."

"Wen?"

Sham lowered her eyes to hide her pride. "Wen will be the name of my lamb. He has opinions."

The herd considered her in silence. They couldn't argue with an unborn lamb who had opinions.

"You are welcome to join us," Dall said. "You and Wen."

"Wen is the most important one now," Mouf said. "Even more important than me."

When no one disagreed with her, she sighed.

Kenir turned to Dall. "Wherever you are going, you must be there in time for Wen. You must be there, wherever it is." To Tuk she said, "Trust the mountain."

WOLVERINE

One by one they entered the forest of treed mountain and found the creek bed.

"Tuk is saving us now, right, Tuk?" Mouf said. "Have you started?"

"He has started," Dall said, and she began to climb.

After a whole winter in the flat valley, it felt good to be climbing again. But soon the bighorn began to lose their nerve, enclosed in the wood without good sight lines, and in territory without the slightest scent of bighorn. They talked together to help them forget the listening, watching silence. As time went on, they slowed down and their talk quieted.

Except for Mouf.

"What is blue mountain like, again?" she asked.

"The stories say man is not there," Tuk answered.

"Is anything there?"

"Of course, Mouf. A mountain, and grassy meadows and rocks and cliffs."

"Story grass? Story rocks?"

"Real rocks. Rocky rocks."

"But if it is just a story, will we have a happy ending?"

"I hope these questions will have a happy ending," Tuk said.

Dall, just ahead of him in the lead, looked back briefly. He could see the weariness in her face. Climbing through the forest was taxing her. It was taxing them all, of course, but going first was the hardest. At least he and the others had the comfort of following, of being in the slipstream of a familiar scent. Still Dall climbed steadily, her head and shoulders bent to the task.

Tuk had lots of time to think about the night wolves, and how the herd had escaped harm because of the trick of climbing on the machines. Speed, agility, and trickery: the law of the peaceable had served him that far. But if not for the gun, he would be bones in the valley.

His horns had begun to grow at a great rate, but not, he thought, fast enough.

A little after midday, long after even Mouf's chatter had ended, the trees stepped back from the banks of the dry creek bed and revealed a small dell. The band stopped, shaking with fatigue, to look for forage, but it was meager and the snow was wet and heavy.

"Are we there already?" Mouf said.

"We are not there, Mouf," Nai said. "We have just begun."

She hung her head. "I shall die of being tired if we have to keep going."

Sham had already made a bed and lay down.

"We have to keep going," Dall said. "But not today. We may not find another clearing before dark. We'll rest and make the top tomorrow, and you are not allowed to die yet, Mouf."

"Tell me when," Mouf said.

Tuk did not sleep well that night. He woke to every sound and wished they had kept going. Early the next morning, though, he could see how the rest and grazing had heartened Sham and Mouf.

Again they climbed. The creek bed became steeper and choked by old growth. Hair lichen hung in pale dry wisps from the trunks of limber pine that crowded with their sharp, naked branches. Dall slowed down. Her footing was hesitant when the creek bed was especially narrow and the trees closed in.

Tuk could hear Rim at the back, encouraging Mouf and Sham, and sometimes nudging them along. He pressed forward, every so often saying to Dall that surely soon the wood would open up again.

Toward afternoon, when Tuk was more weary than he had ever been, the trees gathered suffocatingly close, and the rocky creek bed cut deep into the mountain.

Mouf stopped suddenly. Ovis and Rim were unable to get around her for the dense underbrush on either side of the trail. "I have to stop," she said.

"Here?" Ovis said.

"Yes," said Mouf.

"Yes, you must stop," said a voice out of the wood.

Tuk looked to his left to see a wolverine in the

bracken beside them. Kenir had taught Tuk that wolverines were proud, unwilling to live close even to their own kind, and could be vicious predators.

"What are bighorn doing here on treed mountain?" the wolverine asked.

"We are going to blue mountain," Mouf said.

"Blue mountain?" the wolverine said with a growl. "But this is my mountain, and if you tread my mountain, you pay a price. So which of you will be my dinner?" The wolverine crept closer. "I promise you my kill methods are most refined, second to none, the result of good breeding and aristocratic stock. You are weary and half-starved and trapped with no place to run, and now the little one may lie down and not be able to rise. Perhaps the rest of you can go on, and she can be my dinner. Surely she cannot survive this journey anyway."

"She declines to be your dinner," Tuk said to the wolverine. "In fact, we are not tired at all."

"I am," said Mouf.

"Mouf," Dall said, "the wolverine will only attack if we are weak or wounded, and you are as strong a young ewe as ever I saw."

"Oh. Good," Mouf said, glancing at the wolverine.

One by one they passed by the wolverine and continued their climb. The wolverine followed in the brush to the left of the creek bed, staying parallel to Mouf.

"Never mind," said the wolverine. "Soon enough you will stumble, little one, and hurt your foot, or fall asleep and wake up only long enough to scream a little before you die. But don't worry. I have manners, and I kill quickly, before I even open you up. I am quite skilled."

"That is a relief," Mouf said.

"Of course, I have made the occasional error in judgment," the wolverine said.

"No one is perfect," Mouf said.

"Don't talk to him anymore," Ovis said.

But the wolverine continued to keep pace with the herd.

"You won't make it," he said. "No, you won't. But go ahead and make me wait for my dinner. Be inconsiderate, if you must. It is the way of your lowly kind. No sympathy at all for the fact that I, the finer breed, haven't eaten anything but mice for days . . ."

"We must stay strong and alert until we get to the top," Dall said. "Tuk will tell you a story, Mouf, one to keep you awake. But he will only tell it if you walk."

"I will tell you the story of the wolverine who troubled Lord Denu," Tuk said as he climbed.

"I love a good story," said the wolverine, following alongside.

In the days when Lord Denu wandered the mountains, a wolverine plagued the first herd. He felled and ate two lambs. The matriarch sent a strong yearling to find Denu and ask him to return from his wanderings to help the herd. Denu came, and by then the wolverine had felled a third lamb.

The wolverine was pleased that the king had returned just to deal with him. It made him feel powerful and important, and he strutted before Denu.

"The mountain gave me tooth and claw and an appetite for flesh. I am the proud wolverine, and I am entitled to eat the lowly sheep."

"You *are* a proud creature," said Denu. "Who are your relations, wolverine?"

"Why, you can tell by my name that I am related to the wolves," said the wolverine, drawing his head up tall.

Denu said, "Ah—no wonder you attack our kind, seeing as you are from wolf stock. But are you sure? I met with a wolf not long ago who denied you were any relation at all."

"What?" cried the wolverine. "I shall bring a wolf to you today who will tell you that I am related, probably a close cousin."

Immediately the wolverine ran away, and for days in his absence the herd lived in peace and the lambs grew stronger and faster.

Finally one day he returned looking thin and bedraggled and with a nose that had a wolf's bite in it.

"I see no wolf cousin with you," Denu said to him.

"Wherever I went the wolves said I was not related to them at all," the wolverine said. "I cannot understand it."

"Well," said Denu, "you will have to go then, for I cannot allow just anyone to cull the herd."

The wolverine's stomach growled. "I have been told I look bearish. Perhaps I am related to the bear!"

"Ah—an impressive creature indeed," Denu said. "If you can bring a bear to testify to this, then of course I will understand why you must cull the herd."

Immediately wolverine ran off, and again the herd was left in peace for many days. All this time the lambs were growing bigger and stronger and quicker.

When wolverine returned he was a starved-looking creature. The wolf bite was badly healed, and across his side were four great claw marks—the slash of a grizzly.

"I cannot understand it at all," said wolverine to Denu. "The bears say I am no relation of theirs, no relation at all."

"That is too bad," said Denu. "But I have done some searching of my own while you were away, and I have found your true relation, your very cousin. Would you care to meet him?"

"Yes, yes, of course," said wolverine,

who was now feeling quite alone in the world.

Denu called, and the wolverine waited.

"Here he comes," Denu said.

"Where? I see no one."

Just then a small, slithering creature ran up to Lord Denu and gazed at wolverine.

"What is this weasel doing here?" said wolverine. "I cannot abide a weasel—sneakish things."

"This," said Denu, "is your cousin."

"Cousin? No, it can't be!"

"I am sorry to say," Lord Denu said, "that it can be, and it is. I am afraid that weasels and their families are not permitted to hunt the noble bighorn. You must go, and if you do not, I shall have to tell all the creatures about your relations."

At that, wolverine tripped and tumbled down the mountain in shame, and was never seen among the herd again.

"What a cruel and distasteful story," the wolverine said to Tuk.

"Related to the weasel," Mouf said with a sad shake of her head.

The creek bed had become broader and less steep as Tuk told the story. He felt a breath of open air.

"A few more steps, and we'll be above the tree line," Dall said.

The wolverine crashed through the trees, keeping up with them. "You must go down the mountain, too," he said. "And I will follow."

Finally, as the sun disappeared, they came out into the open, a small rocky clearing on the eastern crown of treed mountain. The sun had been warm on the shadeless clearing and the snow was melting away in spots. They grazed hungrily.

Soon they were more tired than hungry, and they began to paw out their beds. They could hear the wolverine in the bracken just below. As the band fell asleep one by one, Tuk saw that Rim and Ovis were awake.

"We will take turns watching," Tuk said. "I'll go first."

In the quiet of the night, Tuk marveled that they had made it to the top of treed mountain. He had not truly believed they would make it even that far.

FOG

Just before dawn Tuk woke and jumped to his feet. A Chinook had blown in during the night, warming the air and melting much of the snow, but now the air was still, and that stillness had woken him. Fog swirled around his feet and slipped like spirit wolves between the trees that ringed the small clearing. He could hear water dripping in the creek bed and the wolverine snuffling in the trees.

Dall was awake also, gazing intently into the woods.

"The wolverine is still out there," Tuk said to Dall quietly.

She nodded. "Out of sight but within smell." The fog muffled all sound and flitted in the bare branches like ghostly birds. “But feel it, Tuk. Spring is at the top of treed mountain! It is as if spring has always been here, waiting for us.”

Sweet coltsfoot had sprung up overnight, the warm stems dimpling the snow. Tuk’s band feasted on them in the still-dark morning, and on the tender blades of new spring grasses. Tuk ate as much as he could, and gradually, though the fog still pooled on the ground, the skies cleared.

Dall came to his side. “Come look, Tuk,” she said.

She led him to the west side of the clearing and they jumped onto a great boulder muscling out of the earth.

To the west, Tuk could see another mountain, not as thickly treed, but higher, and spotty with meadows among the forests.

“Another mountain,” Dall said, shaking her head. “With forests.”

“But some meadows,” Tuk said. Below them, between treed mountain upon which they stood and meadow mountain in the distance, a valley cupped the fog like a great white lake. The fog shifted and stirred but gave no clues as to what was beneath. At the north end was a break in the fog, and there they could see a river pouring into the valley, split into two shallow arms. At the south end they could see the river flow into a corridor between low mountains.

"Look, Dall, beyond meadow mountain." The peak of blue mountain had just appeared above a bank of cloud, like an island in water. "Do you see it?"

Dall looked and her mouth opened. "Yes, I see it! But—it floats. How can we live on a mountain that floats?"

Tuk and Dall searched out another creek bed going down the west side of treed mountain. When they found it, it was slick with water, but passable for steady bighorn feet.

When they returned to the band, Mouf said, her mouth full of grass, "I smell that wolverine. It makes my food taste funny."

Tuk thought he could smell wolf, too, but perhaps it was only a memory stuck in his nose.

Down they walked, down and down treed mountain, and behind them the wolverine followed, plodding and relentless.

After a long day of miserable trekking, finding little more to eat, they finally came to a grassy area more than halfway to the bottom. They could smell water and something rank coming up from the valley, but the trees blocked their view.

"We'll stay here tonight," Dall said.

"In the trees again?" Mouf asked.

"Mouf," Nai said irritably, "be still. You're making me jumpy, startling at every little thing."

"We are all a bit jumpy," Dall said. She and Sham scraped out their beds beside Mouf. Tuk and Rim and Ovis again took turns to watch. Though they could smell the wolverine skulking nearby, he did not close the gap he had maintained all day.

BEAR

When the sun rose the next day, the band finished the short trek to the flats and emerged from the trees. The wolverine followed, keeping the same measured distance he had kept the day before. Tuk, last in line, felt his haunches quivering, imagining the wolverine's claws in his back.

In the near distance was a fast river. A pair of white owls floated silently on the air to the north as the band approached the banks. Snow melted and fell into the water chunk by chunk. Shining fish darted just above the ice-scrubbed stones of the bottom.

"We will have to cross it," Dall said. "It's shallow enough here, I think."

"Yes, when I am ready," Mouf said.

Dall shook her head. "We must cross it today for the sake of Wen. We must be at the lambing cliffs of blue mountain in time for Sham to have her lamb."

"Wen is the important one," Mouf said. She sniffed. "Something smells bad. Worse than wolverine."

Dall stepped into the water and then stopped, stiff-legged, as a great rise of earth suddenly came to life. It had not been earth at all, but an enormous old bear. He stood on hind legs and looked at them from the opposite bank of the river. His head was boulder-sized and his paws had claws like tree branches.

The bear licked his lips as Dall stepped back out of the water. The band lined up along the bank.

"Sheeps!" the bear called, falling onto all fours. "My river. You step in, I eat."

"You can't own the whole river," Rim said.

"Part," old bear said. "This part. Step in, find out."

"You can't eat us all," Tuk said.

"Just one. Which?" said the bear. He laid his head down on his soddy paws and stared.

"The little one's mine!" the wolverine called from behind them.

"Now what do we do?" Rim asked the others.

"The bear knows we can run back up the creek bed if he comes after us," Tuk said, "so he won't cross the river. Maybe he'll get hungry and go away."

They drank from the river and rested on the east bank, but hours later the old bear had not gone away. He fished a little and found grubs under rocks, but mostly he gazed at the band and drooled. Once they heard a mouse squeal and the scuffling of the wolverine.

"Why does the bear want to eat us when he can eat fish and grubs?" Mouf asked.

Tuk told her what Kenir had taught him about the bear.

> When the mountain made the bear, she asked him, "What would you like to eat, bear?"
>
> "All," said bear.
>
> "All? You want to eat grass and leaves?"
>
> "Yes," said bear. "And meat."
>
> "And meat also?"

"Yes," said bear, "and bugs and berries and bighorn."

The mountain said, "Denu, the bear wants to eat your kind."

Lord Denu considered. Then he said, "The bighorn were given all we wished, and we are happy. But sometimes getting all you wish for is not always best."

"All," said bear. "I wish all."

The mountain gave the bear his wish.

The bear ate grass and leaves and bugs and berries and fish and meat—everything. Sometimes he even ate bighorn. Many, many years passed and the bear grew fat, but still it was not enough. One sad day he found man's garbage. As foul as it was, the bear was wild to eat it. So he feasted, and as his belly got bigger his dignity got smaller. He became familiar with man. An animal cannot be familiar with man unless he becomes his slave. Since bear was too wild to become slavish, man killed him. The bear, who could eat the world, shrank in numbers and spirit, and lost his place as one of the noblest of animals.

The band looked sadly at the bear, who had sniffed morosely through the story.

"Come, sheeps," the bear said. "Come give old bear just a lick of liver."

"It is hard to feel sorry for a bear who wishes to eat our livers," Nai said.

"What is a liver?" Mouf asked.

"I don't know," Rim said, "but it sounds like something I need to be happy."

"It is a part of you," said Ovis.

"Yes, part," said old bear. "Step in, I eat part."

Dall said, "We will cross elsewhere." And she led them away.

The bear called after them, "Sheeps, sheeps!" as the band wandered south along the river. As soon as they were out of the bear's sight, the river deepened and the band sensed dangerous undercurrents. The bank's underbrush became impassable and they could go no farther. Still the wolverine followed.

Dall turned back the way they had come, and they followed her until they had returned to the shallows and the old bear. He called out to them, but they ignored him and walked north. Again the river became deep and uncrossable, and the bank's underbrush too dense to penetrate.

"That is why he fishes there. It is the best place," Dall said.

Ever the wolverine followed at the same distance behind, out of sight in the trees but never out of smell. The band returned to the shallows and the bear, and once again lined up along the bank of the river. The afternoon was wearing on.

"Liver for crossing river," the old bear said. "Come, let me gnaw and nibble, just one . . ."

With the wolverine at his back and the bear at his front, Tuk's belly was as icy as the river. His horns itched and pained. The river rushed over the rocks and the snow-crusted ice fell into the water with a splash.

"If we crossed," Tuk said, "most of us could outrun him. But not Sham, and probably not Mouf."

Dall nodded her head in weary agreement.

"I want to fight him," Tuk said.

"Tuk wants to give the bear his liver," Mouf said evenly to Dall.

What good was speed and agility in the high places going to do them now, Tuk wondered. Of course, there was always trickery. He thought for a time and then said, "I might have a plan."

"Plan?" said old bear. "I eat plan."

"Tell me," said Dall.

"He's listening. You must trust me, Dall."

Dall hesitated, and then nodded.

Tuk called out, "Old bear, if you will let the others cross and go on, I will give you one bite of one part of me. After that, you must let me go."

Dall gasped.

Mouf said, "That's nice of you, Tuk."

"First I bite part?" the bear called. "Then you go?"

"Yes," Tuk answered. "Not all. One bite of one part. Then you let me run away."

"Ha," said the bear. "But if you don't run, I eat all."

"Go now," Tuk said to the others. "When you are on the other side, keep going until I catch up to you. Mouf and Sham, you must run as fast as you can."

"What are you thinking?" Dall asked.

Tuk, knowing the bear could hear everything, said, "Go, and don't look back."

Dall shook her head, and, with a low-stretch bow to Tuk, stepped gingerly into the river. The other ewes followed, and old bear watched them, salivating. Rim and Ovis stayed with him until the last.

"Go with them," Tuk said to his mates.

"No," Rim said.

"It will do them no good to get to blue mountain with no rams," Tuk said.

Ovis nodded and crossed behind the ewes. On the opposite bank he looked back, hung his head, and continued through the brush after the ewes.

"Now you, Rim," Tuk said.

Rim said nothing, and neither did he move.

Together the two young rams stepped into the river.

"We made bargain," old bear said. "Animals speak true."

Tuk said, "Yes, animals speak true. One bite of one part."

A string of drool suspended from the bear's mouth to his paw. "After one bite, you don't feel good. You don't run away. I get liver."

Slowly Tuk and Rim made their way across the cold river. Slowly they climbed from the river onto the bank and faced the old bear. He was as big as two king rams together, his teeth like a row of little horns.

Tuk heard the wolverine behind them splash into the river. He would want to make sure he got his share of a bear kill.

"Ewes be back soon when they come to bog," the old bear said.

"Bog?" Tuk said.

"Now part," said old bear, chomping and lumbering toward Tuk and Rim.

"I didn't say which part yet," Tuk said, holding his ground. "I get to choose, as we bargained."

"Yes, part, part, which part?" old bear growled happily. "Leg? Shoulder?"

"Horn," Tuk said, lowering his head.

Old bear stopped in his tracks. "Horn? Horn not tasty and drippy with blood. Horn dry and crunchy."

"Take a bite from one of my horns, as we bargained. Then you must let us go."

Old bear growled and bared his teeth. Tuk heard more splashing in the river. The wolverine was coming closer.

"I eat anyway," old bear said.

"Animals speak true," Tuk said. "We had a bargain."

"My river," old bear said. "I eat what follows you."

In a movement as quick and slick as a fish, the bear was up and in the water. The wolverine opened his mouth to show his long teeth, and as Tuk and Rim vanished into the brush, bear and wolverine fought tooth and claw.

OTTER

The ewes and Ovis leaped and ran to Tuk and Rim as they emerged from the trees on the west side of the river. Rim told them how they had escaped the bear as they continued walking west, away from the river. They laughed to hear the story. Tuk said to Dall, "Old bear said something about a bog ahead."

"Bogs are mostly shallow," she said hopefully.

"We might be able to find another way," Tuk said. "But—" He stopped and then said very low, "I am sure now. White wolf has picked up our trail and follows us. Can you smell him, Dall?"

"I can."

"Perhaps a bog would discourage a bear or a wolverine or a wolf," Tuk said.

The bog was a great emptiness stretching out between them and meadow mountain. Listless water spread over the valley floor and clumps of weeds reached desperately out of the water, as if to keep from drowning. In places an orange scum bubbled on the surface. On leafless trees, long ago drowned, gray plates of fungus grew, frilled and white at the edges. Cloud shadow shifted over the surface water, making Tuk think of dark creatures beneath.

"So this is a bog," said Rim.

They stood and stared and twitched away the mosquitoes that whined in their ears.

"Maybe we should go around," Nai said.

Dall said, "If we go through, our scent may be lost in the water."

"We can swim," Tuk said, "if it's not too far." But as he surveyed the bog, he knew it would be too far. The bottom, from what he could tell, was clogged with drowned deadwood.

"Wen disagrees with bogs," Sham said, shaking her head.

Dall stared at the expanse of still water as if she did not know how to begin.

"Perhaps we could ask him," Mouf said. "He has been watching us for some time."

They followed her gaze and saw an otter sitting on a little ark of sticks and debris. He had a coat slick as dark ice.

Seeing that they had discovered him, the otter came closer. "What kind of animal are you?" he asked.

"We are the bighorn," Tuk said, dropping his head in a brief bow.

"But your horns are not big."

"We—the males—will have big horns someday," Tuk said. "We are only yearlings."

"We mean to cross the bog," Dall said.

"A bog has channels that you can't see," the otter said, grinning. "Deep parts, but also shallow parts that are thick with weeds and creepers. And sometimes quicksand."

"Wen disagrees with quicksand," Sham said.

"I have never seen creatures like you before," said the otter. "It is boring in a bog. Nothing happens, nothing at all. Oh, you know, your usual death by predator, but other than that— No female otter will come be my mate in such a boring place. But if I help you cross the bog, what a story it would make."

"We would be grateful for your help," Dall said.

"Follow me. I know where the water is shallow and the footing easier," the otter said. "You won't have to swim much, and I hope I won't lead you through quicksand."

"Are you ready?" Dall asked the band.

Each one nodded.

The otter slid off his twiggy ark and into the water, light as a leaf. "Not a single female otter nearby to see this," he complained.

Dall stepped into the bog to follow him.

The otter chattered ceaselessly, and somehow the dark bog seemed less forbidding because of it. Sometimes he would stop to fish or to float. Once in a while he got a little too far ahead, but still Tuk could hear him chattering: ". . . all the river females will want to hear about this, all of them, even the prettiest . . ."

Mostly they were in the water only to their knees, and at times only to the tops of their feet. Twice they had to swim, but only a short way.

As late afternoon became evening, Tuk had almost reached his limit, and he knew Sham and Mouf would be exhausted. When dark began to fall, they were still a distance from the opposite side of the bog.

The otter had swum far ahead.

"Otter, come back!" Tuk called.

"It is time for sleep," the otter called in reply. "I will come back at first light and lead you the rest of the way. Don't worry, you're safe here. That is, you are safe if you don't move. One step to the left or the right, and you could be caught in the weedy bottoms or the quicksand."

"Otter, please . . ." Dall called, but he was gone.

In the day the bog had been dark and driftwood floated like bones beneath the surface, but in moonlight the water shone white and flat as a field of snow. After a time the wind came with shrill whistles that fell into Tuk's ears like burrs, a wind with teeth and wings. He swung his head to fight it.

"Bats," Dall said quietly.

When the moon was almost directly overhead, a chilling howl echoed out of the dark, followed by a watery moan floating over the surface of the water.

"It is the white wolf," Tuk said after a silence. "He has made a kill."

"It's good we came by way of the bog so the wolf cannot reach us," Dall said.

Somehow it helped Tuk to know that, though they were cold and stiff and sore and tired, at least the wolf could not get at them in the bog.

The band stood trapped on their sunken island, hour after hour, starting when beavers smacked the water with their heavy tails, then sinking into a soggy near-sleep.

Once Sham said, "Wen is brave."

Later Mouf fell into the deeper water to her right and came up sputtering and scrambling for their underwater island. "I fell asleep," she said. "Now I am awake."

Mostly the night was long and silent. Tuk could hear, in their silence, everyone hoping the otter really would come back. Still the reeds rattled in the wind. Still the stars swelled and shrank and burned cold.

Finally, when Tuk thought he must sleep in the water whether he drowned or not, he saw in his side vision a gleam of pale light.

"Dawn," Rim said with relief. "We've made it through the night."

Soon the otter came swimming to them. "You're still here!" he called.

"Where did you think we would be?" Tuk asked sharply.

"I wondered if I had imagined you," the otter said. "Come along, come along. I am cheerful today. I slept so well, dreaming of my mate. I have named my bog 'bighorn bog.' "

And so he chattered as they followed him to the west shore of the bog.

When at last they reached firm soil they stood trembling and weary.

"Try not to thank me," the otter said as they fell to grazing.

"I shall try not to butt you," Tuk said.

"Do you know a good way for a bighorn to go up meadow mountain, otter?" Dall asked.

The otter said grandly, "Yes, I do. And I will tell *you* and not *him*. That twisty path there is the long way. And that broad avenue through the trees is the hard way, also called the bee path. And now it is best I go before you get boring."

The otter slipped into the water and emerged again far out in the bog. "I am off to find a mate!"

REST

Spring had deepened on the other side of the bog. Bees and black butterflies rose from the high grasses. The herd dried their coats in the shy warmth of the spring sun, then bedded down as far from the bog as they could make their weary bodies go. They slept most of the day away.

When Tuk awoke in the evening, the sun was low and gold and a warm breeze ruffled the surface of the bog. The rest of the herd was feeding on unflowered buffalo beans when Tuk joined them. As he grazed, he searched out the two paths up the mountain that the otter had shown them.

"So one path is hard and one is long," Rim said, joining him.

"It is hard to go long," Tuk said.

"It is long to go hard," Rim said.

"He said the broad path was the bee path. What do you think he meant by that?" Tuk asked.

"I don't know. We can stay here for a few days and think about it."

Mouf, overhearing them, said, "That is a good idea, Rim. I like that plan better than Tuk's plans, which have bogs and blue mountains in them."

"Mouf," Sham said, "are you forgetting Wen?"

"Oh, yes," Mouf said sadly. "Wen. The most important one."

"We will take one path or the other at dawn," Dall said.

Then, from the north side of the bog, a wolf howl rose and took a bite out of the sky.

The band bunched together. "He hasn't given up. He's going around the bog," Ovis said.

Again the wolf howled, long and slow and hungry.

"He's traveling faster than we are," Ovis said. "Even going around the bog, he could close in tomorrow."

The band stood quietly for a long time. Finally Tuk swallowed a mouthful of dry sedge.

"We have to split up. Dall, you and the band go up one trail. I will go up the other. He will follow me, and you can get away . . ."

Tuk's words were braver than his heart, but he was glad he said them.

"It is a good idea," Dall said to the ground, "for the safety of the band and Wen."

Mouf said, "But—!"

"We will take the long way," Dall said firmly.

"You should leave now and sleep higher on the mountain," Tuk said. "I will leave in the morning to be sure my scent is the easiest to find and follow. Wait for me one full day and one full night. If I don't come, go to blue mountain without me."

Mouf looked at Tuk and then Dall and then Tuk again. Dall laid her head on Tuk's neck for a moment, then slowly turned away. She led the band toward the narrow twisty path.

Rim stayed behind. "If you insist on making new stories," he said, "I want to be in them."

Again the wolf howled, and the air shivered like water in a cold breeze.

BEE TREES

In the morning, Tuk and Rim laid down heavy scent at the beginning of the hard trail so the wolf would know which way they had gone. Then they began the climb up meadow mountain.

As the otter had promised, the path was wide and rocky at first, and they progressed quickly. Still, it felt slow, given that they had a wolf on their heels. The wolf's scent became stronger as the day wore on, he was traveling so swiftly.

Tuk wished he had big horns to fight the wolf. Also he was grateful for the companionship of his peaceable friend and wished he could be more like him. *What kind of animal are you?* Balus had asked. Tuk felt like there were two paths to the answer: one was the long way, and one was the hard way, but he didn't know which was the better way. He reminded himself of Kenir's counsel to trust the mountain.

Late in the afternoon, the wood began to close in and the way narrowed until Tuk and Rim had to walk single file. They came to a part of the wood that was diseased, the tree branches gray as shed antlers. Scattered along the trail were the remains of a rabbit kill. It was an unhealthy place, and gloom followed them like the cloud of gnats that had discovered them in the heat of the day.

Tuk stopped in the path before a curtain of thick brush. "Do you hear that, Rim?"

"Hear what?"

Tuk peered into the brush. "I think I see a way that the wolf could be reasoned with."

"It's a wolf, Tuk. They don't reason with us. They eat us."

"Kenir says the bighorn live in the high places where no other animal wants to live," Tuk said. "We survive on the steeps and on the bare-rock outcrops, and we escape our predators with speed and agility. We go into places others cannot follow. I think we've found such a place."

He stepped aside so Rim could see through the curtain of brush.

The wood and overgrowth opened up to a meadow thick with clover and bright with wildflowers. But rising up from the clover and flowers were many leafless trees, their trunks black with old sugar, having long ago died with honey in their hearts. Droning between the trees were bees, thicker than the mosquitoes on the bog.

Rim stumbled backward at the sight, and that small sound caused the bees to swarm. The earth and air thrummed as the bees readied themselves to guard their ancient treasure.

Rim made a low, guttural sound in his throat, half fear, half fascination.

"Look beyond the trees, Rim," Tuk whispered at his flank, "to that steep rocky rise beyond the field. There—you see the waterfall? After we run through the field, we'll climb the rock tumble at the side of the waterfall all the way up to that cave under the upper falls. The wolf cannot climb that. We'll hide from the bees in the cavity until they go away. From there we'll reach the top and make our way south to meet the others."

Rim whispered, "To go through that field would be to die."

"If we are fast, if we run through the meadow as only the bighorn can, we can make it through in four leaps. If we're fast. And if we don't fall."

"Bighorn can't outrun a wolf," Rim said.

"No, but we can outclimb him. That rock wall west of the bee field is the mountain's gift to us."

"Would white wolf be so foolish as to follow us into the meadow?" Rim asked. "Or do you mean not to tell him? That would not be . . . peaceable."

"I will tell him about the bee trees," Tuk said. He raised his nose. "He's coming."

Tuk could hear the wolf's footpads now, untiring. He could hear the wolf panting.

"Steady," Tuk said.

White wolf appeared below them on the path and stopped cold. He stared at the young bighorn.

"You have given up," he said. "You wish for me to end your fear and suffering."

"Wolf," Tuk said, trying to steady his voice, "you

must stop following us. We are going to blue mountain where it is too forbidding and wild even for the wolf."

"Very well. I will follow you no longer. I will eat you instead."

"We are going to run into the meadow behind us, and there you will not want to follow. It is full of bees."

"Bees? Wolves do not fear bees."

"Many bees. You would best turn back."

"The mountain decrees that some of you must feed me," white wolf said, the fur on his neck lifting. "And you, who called me dog and got my mate killed, are what I hunger for. I will follow you wherever you go."

"Goodbye, white wolf," Rim said.

"Goodbye," white wolf said, and he ran at them.

"Leap!" Tuk cried.

Tuk and Rim turned. With a single great bound they were a quarter the way through the bee field, a quarter the way to the safety of the rocks.

A silence among the bees. A stillness—a disbelief.

"Leap!" Tuk called again. With the second leap,

they were halfway through the bee trees, and the wolf had entered the clearing, drooling, baying triumphantly.

The bees' low steady thrumming became a roar. Tuk heard the wolf cry out with dismay.

The bighorn rams leaped the third time, over and between fallen trees. The bees swarmed Tuk so that he could see Rim only as a shadow beside him. They stung him everywhere, especially on the tender parts of his mouth and eyes and nose. Behind him white wolf howled and snarled in pain and fury.

Leap!

One moment the air was black with bees, and in the next they were on the rock tumble at the side of the fall. Tuk and Rim climbed the fall desperately. As they climbed the air thinned of bees, until finally they were able to duck under the shelf of rock that was the lip of the waterfall. Over the sound of the rushing water they heard white wolf scrambling at the rocks below, falling back, scrambling and clawing again while he howled and whined.

Finally he fell silent.

Tuk and Rim stood behind the waterfall until

the field lightened and the bees returned to their honey business.

They didn't speak. They dipped their swollen nostrils and mouths and eyes into the icy water.

When it began to get dark, Tuk said, "Let's go."

They nimbly climbed the rock tumble beside the waterfall until they reached the top. Far above the bee trees they teetered on little shelves of stone, panting. Their stings burned, and they soothed them again and again in the cold, rushy water.

MEADOW MOUNTAIN

Tuk and Rim bedded down for the night farther up the river that fed the waterfall. The next morning their stings had swollen their eyes almost shut. It was painful to graze. A mild wind blew through a curved blue sky as they made their way up and south on the mountain, looking for Dall and the others.

The wildlife was more abundant on meadow mountain than it had been on treed mountain. Through swollen eyes Tuk saw elk and deer, coyotes and badgers, and birds of every kind. He could still catch the scent of man in his nose when the wind blew down the mountain.

They traveled slowly, stopping often to rest. Gradually they were able to eat a little and the pain in their faces lessened.

At evening, they spied the rest of the band.

The others, when they saw Tuk and Rim approaching, leaped about and ran to meet them. As they came closer, they slowed and stopped and looked tenderly at Tuk's and Rim's swollen noses.

"Are you dead?" Mouf asked.

"Mouf," Dall said, not taking her eyes off Tuk. "You can see they are alive."

"But are your faces dead?" Mouf asked.

"Our faces met with some angry bees," Rim said.

"Bees?"

"Yes," Tuk said. "We may not look so well, but white wolf won't trouble us anymore."

Dall showed them the small mountain meadow they had found, and they all grazed on the new spring grasses. But though their stomachs were full for the first time since they'd left their old mountain, and though the night was mild, and though the scent of the wolf was gone, none of them slept easily.

* * *

When he woke the next morning, Tuk saw Ovis standing beside a pika and his treasure of winter seeds.

"Why are you here?" the pika asked.

"We are going west to blue mountain," Ovis answered.

"I've heard," answered the pika, "that all the animals who go to blue mountain fall off the edge of the world."

"Did you hear that, Tuk?" Mouf said. "The part about falling off the world?"

A mule deer coming down the mountain stopped to speak to them.

"Are you going up the mountain for man's flowers?" he asked.

"No," Ovis said. "We are going to blue mountain, where we can be free of man."

"Man has an outpost farther up this mountain," said the deer. "We go at night to eat the soft grass and the fruit and flowers."

"But doesn't man hurt you?" Nai asked.

"Sometimes," the deer said, turning away, as if Nai had said something impolite. "It is the price of fruit and flowers. Are you the ones who have brought the puma?"

Tuk looked at his bandmates, but none of them appeared surprised. He had smelled puma coming from the south since he'd arrived in the meadow, and now he saw that the others had as well, though no one wanted to say it.

"She has left Kenir's herd to follow us," Dall said.

"Wen disagrees very much with pumas," Sham said.

"She will follow us to blue mountain," Nai said miserably.

"Perhaps it is not even our puma and she will go away," Dall said.

Tuk knew it was, but he did not say.

All that day they grazed the spring grass and felt they could not go up or down. They had a puma at their backs and man ahead on their trail.

That night, as if she knew they had become aware of her, the puma screamed the white out of the moon until it was tattered and gray. Tuk felt an urge to scream back at her.

"Blue mountain will not be as good with a puma eating us one by one," Mouf said.

"We could fight her together," Tuk said.

"Tuk, you know we can't fight the puma," Dall said.

"We could fight her, but we don't because we are weak and afraid," he answered.

Dall raised her head slowly until it was very high and her eyes met his. She spoke in a soft, even voice. "Since the beginning of the mountain, our kind chose peace, and for time and time we thrived. Now the world is changing, and will we change with it? Or will we allow ourselves to die? Perhaps you will make a new kind of bighorn. But do not accuse me of weakness and fear if I choose the other way."

Tuk knew that Dall's gentleness had always come out of strength. That was why they all loved her. That was why he loved her.

He knew that his need to fight came out of fear, fear that the mountain didn't care, that the story of their band would end badly. One of his horns was full of temper, and the other knew that if he went to blue mountain as he was, he would be infecting it with something worse than pumas.

"Pumas fear nothing but man," Ovis said. "That is what her scream said. She does not even fear the high cliffs. Nothing but man, and sometimes the puma eats a man just to swallow her fear."

When some time had gone by and no one had fallen asleep, Tuk said, "What if we went to the outpost and stayed there until our scent was completely disguised by man scent? She might lose the trail or turn back."

Dall sighed from deep in her belly. "It is a good idea. In the morning we will climb in the direction of the outpost."

The starlings were chattering with one another and the sun promised warmth when the band set off up the mountain to the outpost.

Sham was big with the lamb growing inside her. She was resolute and never complained, but she frequently told them Wen's opinions about hunger and sore feet and fatigue and flies and especially pumas.

The outpost, when they finally came to it, turned out to be a shelter made of killed trees stacked upon one another. It had the familiar scent of man on it—fire and salt and metal—but not as overpowering as Tuk remembered from man in the winter valley. The outpost had a woodsy smell, a natural smell that was mildly reassuring.

They saw the trees and flowers the deer had spoken of, but the bighorn were not tempted by anything to do with man. The band stayed only close enough to be within the wash of man scent. The scent of the puma was soon driven out of their nostrils, and Tuk knew that meant the puma could no longer smell them, either. Together they talked of how they would leave the next day, drenched in the scent of man, and with luck be at the top of meadow mountain by evening.

There they hoped to have a close view of blue mountain for the first time.

When they bedded down, Mouf said, "What if blue mountain isn't there, Tuk? What if it's just a story and the story is that Mouf and her friends and most important Wen all fell into a blue mountain nothing and at the bottom of the nothing was the throat of a huge puma? What if?"

NET

In the night, the pop of a gun.

Up!

Around him Tuk's bandmates leaped up.

Up!

But Tuk could not get up.

"Tuk! Run!" Dall cried.

But he could not move. The more he struggled to get up, the less he could move.

Something bound him like a great spider's web. The gun had shot a net over him.

In another moment he saw a man, and another, and one more. They came closer until they touched him.

Flee! Flee! Tuk told himself, but the more he struggled against the web, the tighter it became.

Two men knelt to bind his forelegs and back legs. One of the men seemed to speak to him in a soft, strange language—tricky sounds, as if he could speak the language of every animal at once. It had the music of birds in it, the buzzing of mosquitoes, the clicks of beetles, the round depth of an elk's call, and the gutturals of a porcupine.

Tuk was helpless, but still he tried to fight. One of the men put a covering over his eyes. Tuk realized that he was not injured, but trapped.

The men continued to make their tricky language, but over it he heard, "I'm here, Tuk."

"Mouf?"

"Yes, I'm here."

"Are you trapped?"

"No. I'm just here."

"Run, Mouf!"

"No. I will stay here with you."

"The men will see you!"

"They see me. They are making their sounds at me, but they aren't trying to trap me."

“Mouf, is that really you?”

“I think so.”

“But—but you are so brave.”

Peaceable Mouf. Tuk could not tell her how it eased his fear to know that she was nearby, that he could smell her familiar scent. He thrashed against the web.

“Don’t fight the web, Tuk,” Mouf said. “It just makes it worse.”

He tried to calm himself.

“Dall? The others?” he asked, panting.

“They are safe,” Mouf said.

He felt as if he were falling from a great height into the dark. He couldn’t fight the web anymore. It had won. He wasn’t sure if a moment or a moon passed. Mouf was closer now, and absolutely still, as if the men were not there making their tricky sounds, sometimes lowing like cows, sometimes bleating like lambs, sometimes tapping like the sound of hail on stone.

“Mouf, what are they doing?”

“They are putting something on your ear.”

Just then Tuk heard a sharp sound in his ear, and at the same time felt a pain. He cried out in surprise.

He felt another sharp pain in his shoulder like a sting, and then he felt sleepy and calm, as if he were dreaming.

"They are taking the web off you now." Mouf sounded far away.

In a few moments he felt the web fall off, and the cover was removed from his eyes. He was awake, aware of everything around him, and yet unable to move. He saw the men closely now, that their faces and arms were naked as newborn mice. Two of them talked to Mouf, who ignored them with great dignity. The other stroked Tuk's side, and he thrilled at this gentleness.

His ear throbbed with the device they had attached to it. In a few moments the men vanished. Mouf put her nose next to his.

"Time to get up, Tuk," she said.

His legs twitched, and he ached as if he had fallen a great way, but he stood up suddenly, shaking.

He leaned against Mouf a little, getting his legs. He sniffed and nudged her.

"This way, Tuk." Mouf led him slowly away from the outpost toward the trees.

Tuk tried twitching his ear as he would to rid it

of an insect, but the device was part of his ear now, cold and heavy. In a short while he saw the others coming toward him, silent as shadows. He was still the same Tuk, a yearling with newly grown horns, but from the look of the others as they came creeping back, he might well have been sporting a set of full-curl horns.

"What have they done to you, Tuk?" Dall said, sniffing at the device.

"I don't know."

"We must go. We must leave this place now, in the dark," Dall said. She began to walk away, and all of them followed.

CLICK!

Even if the puma had followed them to the outpost, they reeked so strongly of man smells now that surely they would be hard to track. She would not give up easily, Tuk knew, but he hoped they had made it more difficult to be found.

It was a long time until dawn, but Dall could not rest. They continued their climb toward the top of meadow mountain. When morning came, still the band made its winding way, wading in broad-leafed undergrowth, in shadow and sun, beneath a roof of leaves and bird call.

From time to time the forest would end and open to untouched meadows, and they would briefly rest and feast and feel the breezes and breathe. Then again the closeness of the forest. The trees bent toward them curiously, almost welcoming, as if they had been waiting for the arrival of bighorn since they were striplings.

When the sun was fully up, they stopped in a meadow where the bones of the mountain jutted out.

The device in Tuk's ear was heavy and itchy, but the worst was the unnerving sense that man was always close by. His nose told him no, but his ear reminded him of guns and nets and man's mesmerizing language.

Tuk wandered a little way from the band. He wished he could be a lamb again who knew nothing of pumas and wolves, guns and nets, and devices that itched and burned and clicked.

Clicked?

He listened.

Nothing. Nothing.

Click.

Some part of Tuk had liked the way the others looked at him with admiration for having been in the hands of man and having escaped. They had stared in amazement at the device, as if it gave him a little of the magic of man.

But now he knew something, and it took the heat out of him. He had not escaped man at all.

The device was speaking to man.

It clicked to tell man where he was.

They were tracking him, just as the puma was.

HOME

After a rest the band continued on its way. Tuk was glad for brave Mouf's chatter so he did not have to listen to the clicks. Now when she asked him questions, he answered agreeably and sometimes asked her a few questions in return.

In the afternoon they came to the top of meadow mountain. It was dotted with trees, but through the trees Tuk saw a rocky crest and, beyond that, the sun-washed sky.

Slowly he walked toward the crest. Slowly he walked through the trees.

Slowly. Slowly.

When Tuk came out of the trees—

When he came out of the trees and stood upon

the crest and saw blue mountain close for the first time—

When he saw blue mountain for the first time in the full light, his heart called it home.

Blue mountain was so high and wide it could not fit in his eyes all at once. It lay like a vast sleeping bighorn, the feet swelling out in a lowland, rising to muscled shoulders, and finally to tundra and horns of rock at the peak. It was a whole world tipped over on its side.

He could see, about halfway up the mountain, a sward already greening up from the snowmelt. That would be where Dall would establish their summer feeding range. Higher still were cliffs for the lambing, and beyond that, he could sense territory for the rams to wander.

It was pristine. It was perfect for the bighorn.

"It's real," Rim said.

"Yes," Tuk said. "Did you doubt it?"

"Yes."

"Me, too," said Tuk. "Sometimes."

All the others gathered to look with wonder at the mountain before them.

"It's not blue anymore," said Tuk. "It's green with

trees and meadows and gray with rock and white with snow, but no blue . . ."

"It is still a *bit* blue," Mouf said.

"A bit," Tuk agreed.

Dall said, "We will stay here tonight. At dawn we will make the descent to the bottom of meadow mountain."

But later, in the quiet dark, the soft click from the device filled Tuk's ear, making it hard to sleep.

In the morning, fog rose like ghostly water around their middles.

"Oh, dear," Mouf said. "Blue mountain has vanished again. Too bad. I guess we have to go back."

She turned around as if she would begin the journey back to their old mountain that very moment. As she did, the puma's scream echoed up the mountain loud enough to make a family of partridges fly out of the fog.

"Go back and you will walk right into the mouth of a puma," Ovis said.

They read the gray air with their noses.

Click.

Tuk said, low and firm, "I must stay behind while you all go on."

All heads rose in alarm, as if the puma had just walked into their midst.

"No, that was before," Mouf said. "That was a good plan for a wolf, but not a puma, right, Dall?"

"I can't go with you anyway, Mouf," Tuk said. "Come close to me and be silent, and you will see why."

They all inched closer. A thrush called.

"Is this a game?" Mouf asked.

"Shhh. Listen. Listen to my ear."

They huddled closer. Again the thrush called.

"You have a bird in your ear?" Mouf asked.

"Hush," Dall said.

Click.

The band jumped back as if the click had been as loud as gunshot. The thrush flew away in a flurry of feathers.

"What was that?" Nai said. "It speaks?"

"No," Dall said solemnly. Tuk watched as understanding crept into her eyes. "It tracks."

"You see why I must not go with you," Tuk said. "We have not made this long journey to escape man only to lead him to us on blue mountain. Since I cannot go, it makes sense that I lead the puma away from you."

His bandmates stared at him.

"Tuk is right," Dall said. "He cannot come like that to blue mountain." She said it as if her tongue were swollen. "For the sake of the herd. For the sake of Wen."

"You know you love him best, Dall," Ovis said, his voice quiet and kind.

She nodded. Tuk felt strange to hear this spoken. It was a secret he had always known but had never told himself. It made him deaf to the clicking sound for a moment.

She raised her head slowly, as if her horn buds were heavy as a ram's. "We must go, now, and without Tuk." She put her mouth close to Tuk's ear. "You see far, Tuk, and you are strong. Maybe—I hope—I am sure you will find a way to come to us. If you trust, the mountain will take care of you."

With that, she turned to walk away.

"Wen is crying," Sham said.

"Wen must be brave, like me," Mouf said, sniffling.

Tuk watched them follow Dall in a line. All but Rim.

"Why should you make all the stories?" Rim said.

PUMA

Tuk and Rim watched the rest of the band until they disappeared into the scrub and made their way toward the peak of meadow mountain.

With the puma following, it seemed strange to Tuk that the sun should be so warm on his horns, its light so kind that he could look almost directly at it.

"Now what do we do?" Rim said.

"We leave a fresh scent leading south and down," Tuk answered. "Away from the direction the others have gone."

Tuk could smell the puma closer now. He could smell her hunger. She had not eaten in a long time. Tuk had not known a puma could smell so desperately hungry.

"Tell me a story, Tuk," Rim said as they walked. "One to pass the time."

"I will tell the story of the cat's eyes," Tuk said.

In the beginning times, Lord Denu saw the suffering of the old and the young and the ill as they fell prey to the big cat. One day he asked the mountain, "Mountain, you have made us happy in every way. Why have you made us suffer when we fall to the claws of the big cat?"

The mountain said, "Go, appeal to the cat and see if he will make the matter more merciful."

So Denu went back down the mountain to speak to the cat. He said, "I come with permission from the mountain to ask you for a boon. When you come to kill, make it merciful and painless, I beg you."

The cat smiled. She had longed to meet the great Denu and take a bite out of his glossy, meaty rump. Now here he was.

"I care not about the pain of your kind,

only the pain in the bellies of my hungry kittens," she said.

As they spoke, Denu saw the cat's eyes up close for the first time. He saw their unearthly stare, and for a moment he forgot himself and was lost in her gaze.

Denu shook himself, then said, "It is good that I was able to break the spell of your great green eyes, cat. If they had been only a little more staring, I might have lain down before you and allowed myself to be eaten. Good day."

Denu walked away, but looked back to see the cat run to mountain, just as he had hoped.

Not long after, the cat came down from the mountain and called to Denu. He went to her, knowing her intent. As he approached her, he saw that her eyes were even larger than before. He felt as though he was falling into the cat's great green eyes as he might into a bay of the river. He saw that she crouched to pounce, but staring into her eyes, he was unafraid. She pounced and sank her teeth into his neck, but he felt no pain.

Just then the mountain came and tossed the cat away from Denu.

"You asked me for more beautiful eyes," said the mountain, "and I came today to find what you have done with my gift. Now I see."

Denu, coming to himself, arose and said to the mountain, "Do not be angry. It has been as I wished. This time I felt no pain, nor any fear, because of the cat's eyes."

The mountain saw the love Denu had for his kind and healed Denu and made it as if he had never been bitten.

Tuk stopped.

He and Rim had gone south a long way and down some, and the ground had been uneven and stony, the trees wizened and thin. Now the forest ended, and so did the earth. Wrapping east around the mountain was a steep, high cliff.

"Trust the mountain," Tuk said to himself.

A voice from behind them hissed, "You think the mountain loves only you."

Tuk turned to see the puma, her long, silky muscles and the bowl of her ribs visible beneath her coat.

"Jump, Rim," Tuk said evenly.

In a spray of leaves and dirt, Rim jumped and found a perch on the bare rock of the cliff. Tuk followed and perched on a narrow shelf of stone.

The puma did not jump. She slunk slowly to the border between trees and cliff. "This time it is not a kitten that hunts you." She stepped onto a ridge in the rock wall as sure-footed, almost, as a bighorn.

Rim and Tuk moved higher.

"You pushed," said the puma.

Rim stepped carefully to a new, higher notch in the cliff. Tuk followed just behind him.

"The mountain gave me tooth and claw to kill anything I find here. The mountain made me also to climb."

Slowly Rim began making his way across the cliff face, picking his footholds carefully, and slowly Tuk followed. At times it seemed the way ahead was smooth as a river pebble, but the moment they needed it, they would find a spot just the size of a bighorn's foot.

The puma snarled and swiped at Tuk, ripping a clump of fur from his flank. It floated into the emptiness below. Rim startled and jumped down to a wide ledge on the cliff.

"Not down!" Tuk cried. He glanced back to see the puma go completely still.

"Go higher, Rim!" Tuk said.

Rim looked about him but didn't move. "I can't see any footholds."

"You I will kill for hunger," the puma said to Rim. "The other for revenge." Tuk saw the muscles in the puma's shoulders ripple into pounce position.

"Rim, you can jump to where I am," Tuk called. "You don't have to see the footholds. Just jump to where I am. There's room."

"What if we can't both fit—"

"Now."

"No!"

"Switch!" Tuk called out, and he leaped down to Rim's ledge, forcing Rim at the same moment to leap up.

Tuk quivered on his ledge, every muscle straining for balance.

In the next moment the puma jumped to the ledge below. Tuk faced her.

He was overpowered by her scent, surprised at her size and strength, seeing her now so close. Her eyes were as green as a spring leaf.

"Tuk," she said, "will you fight me as you did my kitten?"

She had almost all the ledge now. In Tuk's left eye was the rock of the cliff, and in his right eye only blue sky and cloud.

"No. My kitten you would fight, but not me. I will kill you, and then your friend. And then I will follow the others."

"The others?" Tuk whispered. "No others. Just me and my friend."

She grinned, and he could see each tooth in her mouth—each one yellow and finely pointed. He bowed his head at the same moment that the puma lunged for his throat. Her teeth, instead of closing on his throat, closed on his ear.

He felt her teeth go through the ear with the device. She jerked at his ear, trying to unbalance him. He heard Rim cry out to him.

Tuk clung to the mountain, held to the rocks beneath his feet while the puma ripped at his ear.

His ear began to tear away from his head. The cat jerked at him, and he held on to the mountain.

He was a bighorn. He endured. Endured the cold and the storms of the high places. Endured the pain of puma teeth ripping off his ear.

Tuk felt his back feet slipping, slipping, slipping—

And then they found a small protuberance in the rock face. He braced against it, and it held.

The puma jerked one more time with all her strength, and lost her balance

and the puma and the ear
and the ear and the puma
and the device fell—
all fell into the emptiness
all to the bottoms below.

The puma snarled and screamed as she fell, and the mountain echoed her cries even after she was silent.

BLUE MOUNTAIN

A day of steady walking through deep alpine herbmats brought them halfway down meadow mountain. A second day brought them to the bottom. On the third day they crossed the valley, lush with alfalfa and vetch and yarrow.

Finally they climbed the lower slopes of blue mountain.

Tuk believed ever after that blue mountain healed him, that the cold, clean air, untainted by man or any scent of predator, was the reason his wound scabbed over quickly. It didn't hurt as much as the constant click of the device had when it had been attached to him.

Tuk and Rim made their way up blue mountain,

stopping only briefly to graze. On the dry rocky slopes, they saw creeping juniper and larch and cliff brake—all clinging to the stone, thriving at the heights, just like the bighorn. Tuk felt that this place and everything on it was proof that the mountain meant for them to have a part of the world as theirs alone.

The next day they came to the foot of a steep-sloping meadow that reached to a high rocky ridge, with clefts in it for shelter from spring storms. Near the top of the meadow, just below where the rock burst out of the soil, they saw their bandmates, and at the same time the band saw them.

They ran and leaped, and one by one they touched noses, except for Mouf.

"Is that really you, Tuk?" she asked.

"It is me."

"Are you sure? Because you know you have only one ear."

Sham, swollen and taut as a ripe berry with her lamb, said, "Yes, it is strange that he has one ear, but Wen would recognize Tuk anywhere."

"But—does the puma follow?" Ovis asked.

"Tuk would not have come had the puma followed," Dall said.

Rim said, "If you will listen, I will tell you the whole story."

And so, with the blue of the afternoon sky deepening to the color of crocus, and the daytime moon poised like a white dandelion ball on the tips of the trees to the south, and the wind blowing warm from the west, Rim told the story of what had happened to them and the puma.

At the end of the story, the band huddled together and nudged Tuk and praised him. Dall did a low-stretch bow.

"You brought us to blue mountain, Tuk," she said. "And when you came you brought peace with you."

Then they ran to explore and play as they had not since they were lambs. That night when they bedded down, Tuk thought an ear a good trade for the gentle way Dall licked his wound just before she fell asleep.

The next morning Sham went to the lambing cliffs alone, for Wen's opinion was that it was time for him to be born.

WEN

During the days that Sham was away, the herd had nothing to do but feast on bromegrass and timothy, sweetgrass and wild oat. They found delicate columbine between the rocks and nibbled on meadow parsnip.

A few days later Sham brought Wen to join the herd, and the ewes greeted him with soft nudges and licks and grunts.

"He is so fine a lamb," Nai said. "So handsome. He has the look of Dos about him."

Mouf moved around him slowly so he would not be frightened away.

"May I keep him?" she said.

"We will share," Sham said.

When Dall approached, the herd turned aside for her.

"Wen," Sham said. "This is the matriarch. Stand tall."

Dall sniffed at him, examined his eyes and ears and feet, and then stood back with a look of approval.

"Welcome to the herd, Wen," she said softly. "Look about you and tell me what you see."

Wen took a long time. He looked at the meadow and the grass and flowers in it, and the great boulders that erupted from the earth, and the cliffs beyond and the valley below.

Finally he said, looking east, "I see a mountain."

Mouf laughed, and Dall hushed her with a look.

"The mountain is all around us, yes," Dall said with care.

"Not this mountain," Wen said. "That one."

They all followed his gaze. Tuk stared over the vast and well-watered valley and beyond to meadow mountain, spotted with sun and green shadow. Beyond that he could see treed mountain as a dark shadow, and beyond that he could see a thin edge of blue sky in the shape of a mountain. The others looked, too, but said they could not see anything but the deep far sky. All but Tuk.

"It is a blue mountain," Wen said.

"Wen," Mouf said. "I will explain it to you. You are standing on blue mountain. It isn't over there, it is under your feet. But don't worry, I will teach you all the important things."

Over the warm summer the band grew sleek and fat on the abundance of blue mountain, and Wen grew quick and strong.

Often when Wen played nearby, Tuk would fall silent and gaze eastward over the valley, in the direction from which they had come.

One day Wen said to Tuk, "You see it, don't you. You can see the blue mountain, too."

Tuk nodded and said, "I will tell you a story about that mountain, Wen. Once there was a beautiful mountain with cliffs and rocks and peaks for climbing, with a fine winter valley, with mineral licks and lodgepole forests and grassy meadows for the ewes and the lambs, and fine rams for the fall. But time came when the herd could no longer live there, when man sheep ate their winter valley, and men built dwellings and trails over their grass, and the wolf and the puma feasted on the dwindling herd. It was a cold, sad time, but a nursery band heard of a far mountain where man did not come. One day as yearlings the band left to find this new mountain. As they did, one in the band promised that he would come back for them. The band found the mountain, and it was just as the stories had said."

"Did he remember to return for the others?" Wen asked.

"He did," Tuk said quietly.

"I know what you're thinking, Tuk," Rim said after Wen had run off. "But the herd had its choice. I'm sorry for them, but it was the wrong one."

"Winter valley will only be worse this year," Tuk said.

"They know where the breach is," Rim answered. "Let them find the way themselves."

"Rim, think of this at least: we are small in number, and our greatest protection is that we live as a herd. Someday predators will come."

Rim sighed. "I will come with you. That is the way our stories go."

JOURNEY TO THE HERD

Tuk and Rim set out. They decided to travel around instead of over meadow mountain and bog valley, around and between their brother mountains that flanked them on all sides. Walking in the trees and shrubbery of the lowlands, they startled at every sound and shadow. Often they smelled man, but they set their noses toward the old valley and made their steady way.

Mornings, they shook off dreams and dark, and found forage. Together they would set out on the journey again.

After many days, they came to a wasteland. For miles all they could see were the blackened remains of trees. On the air was the lingering and choking smell of smoke. The wind blew ashes over the narrow shadows of the standing trunks.

"At least it affords long sight lines," Tuk said.

A howl shuddered over the hills, and watchful ravens turned their heads as Tuk and Rim entered the burnt forest.

They trod out the miles in silence. Tuk seemed to not be able to remember a single story. He felt sometimes that he had dreamed blue mountain, that he had dreamed the herd. Only Rim's constant presence kept him going.

When it was too dark to see, they slept in a pocket of dry ground where two fallen trunks had made a small recess in the earth. In the morning they thought they could see the shadow of trees in the distance. They walked a little faster and often raised their noses to catch the scent of living pine.

Toward evening, just as they came to the end of the burnt forest, the gray clouds above shredded and the sky opened wide and blue.

"Do you smell it, Rim?"

"The pines?"

"Yes, but do you smell the other thing?"

Rim raised his nose. "Winter valley."

* * *

More man dwellings had been erected in the valley over the summer, one as tall as the ancient trees. They saw more machines and man trails and more fences. Tuk and Rim crossed the road and began the climb to the summer meadow. They came to the stone outcropping that overlooked the valley and walked through trees up the trail that had the smell of generations of bighorn. Finally they came over the steep rocky face to the stand of pines and the small creek. They could smell the herd.

Tuk and Rim knew they made a thin, sore sight when they finally approached the herd, but the herd looked little better. Though they had had a summer in the meadow, their range had been cut off by the forest fire, and their vigilance against predators had made them thin and tattered.

No one seemed to remark upon their approach. The herd grazed without energy. They had no curiosity about the newcomers, nor had the rams that hovered on the outskirts of the herd. Tuk knew the rams would have been forced to stay close to the main herd because of the fire.

"Please tell me where I might find Kenir," Tuk asked Zel, one of Balus's bandmates.

"Who are you?"

"I am Tuk, and this is Rim. We have returned to lead you to blue mountain."

"You are not Tuk," she said, addressing him. "Tuk died."

"I did not die. I am here, and the band who left with me also is alive on blue mountain. It is more wonderful than we imagined, and the stories that man is not there are true."

Zel came closer. "Tuk and the others went to blue mountain which wasn't true and they dropped off the world."

Rim said, "If I were dead, I would tell you."

"Rim wasn't so big as you," Zel said.

Another ewe stepped forward and sniffed nervously in their direction. "Tuk had two ears," she said shortly.

"Yes, two ears." The others nodded.

"Ask Kenir, the matriarch," Tuk said. "Ask my once-mother, Pamir."

"Tuk," said Kenir, breaking through the herd. She looked him up, down, and around.

"I am sorry to tell you, Tuk, that Pamir died of lungworm, along with some others." She walked around him and Rim, as if to be sure they were real. "So blue mountain is not just a story."

"It is just as the stories said, though," Tuk said. "It is beautiful."

"And the others?"

"They are well, including Wen."

Kenir said quietly, "I have looked for you every day. Now you are saving us, Tuk." She turned to the herd. "We leave for this blue mountain at Tuk's word."

"I knew it was Tuk," Zel said. "I knew it was him all along."

The rams had watched and listened from a distance, and soon Tragus, now the king ram, made his way to Tuk. "So it is true—you found the way to your blue mountain?"

"Yes, sir," Tuk said.

Tragus nodded slowly. "My friend Dos would have been pleased. When the herd leaves, the rams will follow."

After Tragus drifted away, Balus and his band-mates approached Tuk and Rim.

When they were within clashing distance, Balus raised his horns and his chest.

"I never expected to see you again, Tuk. I thought you had gone to join a herd of your own kind, whatever that was."

Tuk thought carefully about what was hiding under his first moment of anger, and was surprised to find sadness. He had told himself many times that it didn't matter what Balus said, but now he knew it did matter. It mattered because the things Balus said were sometimes what Tuk had thought of himself.

But now he knew he was a bighorn, that he belonged to the mountain and to the peaceable.

"Blue mountain has room enough for every kind of bighorn, Balus," Tuk said.

Balus glanced at his bandmates.

"Kenir has said we leave for blue mountain in the morning," Tuk said to him, "and I would like your thoughts. Would it be better for us to leave tomorrow, or should we wait another day to see how the weather goes?"

Balus glanced again at his mates, who kept their eyes on Tuk.

"Tomorrow," Balus said.

"Then it will be tomorrow," Tuk replied.

Balus's mates dipped their heads to Tuk and walked away. When he realized they were leaving, Balus turned and followed, with one puzzled backward glance to Tuk.

OLD FRIENDS

Tuk and Rim decided that the way they had come around the mountains was both longer and harder, so they said nothing when Kenir led the herd down into the winter valley and toward the breach in treed mountain.

The herd was quiet when they saw the creek that climbed to the top. The spring melt had altered the stones some, but now in late summer the way was passable again. A slick of icy water could not stop a bighorn. Rim walked near the head of the line, behind Kenir, and Tuk at the end, behind the rams. Tuk remembered the journey up treed mountain, so, though he was bigger and stronger this time, he was patient with the stragglers.

On the second day the line came to a stop. Tuk made his way to Kenir at the front. She was gazing into the underbrush at a wolverine.

"It's our old friend," Rim said. "I see you escaped the old bear."

"I welcome you all to my mountain," said the wolverine. "Which of you will be my dinner? I promise you, my kill methods are most refined, second to none, the result of good breeding."

"Hello, wolverine," said Tuk.

"Have we met before?" the wolverine asked, eyeing Tuk's horns.

"We have. I am Tuk."

"Tuk!" The wolverine squinted. "Never heard of you. Never heard of that Mouf either, whom I would never eat no matter how hungry."

"We thank you for your kindness in allowing us to climb . . . your mountain," Tuk said. "An animal from such stock as yourself, appearing to be cousin to the noble wolf or the great bear, would surely allow safe passage to a hungry herd of bighorn."

"Wolf," murmured one in the herd.

"Bear," murmured another.

The wolverine blinked.

Finally he said, "Ah, yes. Tuk. I remember you after all, I think. You were smaller then, and you had more ears, and you were not nearly as polite."

"Yes," Tuk said.

The wolverine twitched and stared, and then said, "This is my mountain, of course, and I . . . I command all the beasts on it to let you continue on your journey unmolested. But I won't be there to distract the old bear at the river for you this time. He left me with a nasty scar to remind me the river is his."

Tuk bowed a small bow.

"Thank you, lord of treed mountain," Kenir said.

Wolverine's fur puffed out. He drew himself up tall and inclined his head grandly as the herd passed by him, each giving the wolverine a small bow. Balus and the yearlings looked from Tuk to the wolverine in respectful silence.

When they had all passed on, Tuk said, "Thank you, wolverine. I am sorry for your empty stomach."

"It is surprising," said the wolverine, "how the word *lord* can fill the belly."

"As long as you keep your kind from blue mountain," Tuk said, "I will tell a new wolverine story to the lambs, one about how the wolverine fought a bear and lived."

"It is done," said the wolverine. "You will never see my kin on blue mountain."

The herd complained only a little about sore feet and poor forage as they made their journey. If one or two got too loud with their complaints, Kenir would say, "Who wants to go back and spend the winter in the old valley?"

When they were a short distance from the river, Tuk instructed Kenir to wait in the trees, back from the bank.

"I smell bear," she said, sniffing the air.

"Yes," Tuk said. "Stay out of sight until I call."

Tuk walked to the bank. The bear was in his spot by the river, yawning. Tuk knew the bear would not be tricked again, and again some of the herd would not be fast enough to escape him. But he had been taught that the herd could be a protection, and so he said, "Old bear, we ask permission to cross your river."

The old bear stood up, sniffing. "We? I see no we. Only one. You. The one who tricks."

"We wish to cross, please."

"*We* must come to me for bites," old bear said. "This time no horn."

"If you bite one, you must bite all of us," Tuk said.

"Yes, come. I bite all."

Tuk stepped into the river, and the bear stood up in anticipation.

"Come," Tuk called to the herd.

Out of the trees stepped the rest of the herd—the lambs, the yearlings, the ewes, and finally the rams. It was not a large herd, but big enough to intimidate one old bear.

"We?" said bear.

"We," said Tuk.

Tuk began to cross the river, and as one the herd also stepped into the shallow water and began to cross, Tragus last of all. As they emerged from the river they faced old bear, looking at him with staring yellow eyes.

With a growl ending in a whimper, old bear sat down.

"No bites?" Tuk said.

"Not hungry," old bear grumbled.

"Goodbye, old bear."

"Mean," old bear said as Tuk and the herd walked away.

When the herd came to the bog, the ewes with lambs in them were exhausted.

"This we cannot cross," Kenir said.

"Not without help," Tuk said. "But help will come."

A sleek female otter swam through the bog toward him.

"Welcome to bighorn bog," she said. "You must be the creatures my mate told me about."

"And what did he tell you?" Rim asked.

"He told me he saved every one of you his very own self from the bog, and that you declared him the king of the bog."

"Did he tell you all that, then?" Rim said.

Just then the otter came swimming up. "Be careful! Come away!" he called to his mate.

"But here are the beasts who love you so," she said, "who made you king of the bog."

The otter looked from her to Tuk and Rim.

Tuk made a low-stretch bow. "King Otter, we

ask for permission and help to cross your bog," he said.

The otter sputtered, and then said, "Brave bighorn, of course you may cross my bog, and of course I will help you. Again."

"And otter, we do not wish to spend the night in the bog."

"A night in the bog! Not at all! I am not sleepy. I am cheerful. You will be across in a short time. Follow me!"

And so the herd crossed, each bighorn following carefully in the footsteps of the one ahead, and Kenir at the front following the otter. The otter was true to his word, and they crossed without incident.

Once on the other shore, Kenir said, "No wonder you made it safely to blue mountain, Tuk—with wolverines and bears so willing to allow, and otters so willing to help."

MEADOW MOUNTAIN AGAIN

When they came to meadow mountain, the herd drifted toward the wide rocky path to the top.

"You don't want to go that way," Tuk said to Kenir. "We will take the narrow twisty path."

"Why?" she asked.

"Wolf bones," Rim said.

Fog hid the twisty path, fog dimmed the day, fog filled the night when they took a wide pass to avoid the man outpost. Their coats dripped with fog, their feet waded in it. When they came at last to the top of meadow mountain, they could not see blue mountain at all—just a world of deep cloud, mottled gray and white.

"So that's what a story looks like," Zel said.

"It is just the fog," Kenir said. "Isn't it, Tuk?"

"Yes," Tuk said. "We'll see blue mountain in the morning."

When Kenir saw blue mountain in the morning—

When the sun burned up the fog, and Kenir and Tragus saw blue mountain—

When they saw blue mountain for the first time, that the long high slopes were green with good grass and that it was vast and beautiful and real, they rejoiced.

"You are a good storyteller, Tuk," Tragus said quietly.

They descended meadow mountain, exclaiming at the beauty of blue mountain whenever the forest afforded them a view. They rested in the new wintering valley for several days. The valley was rich with good food, and in a single moon cycle the herd grew sleeker and fatter, their eyes lost their hollow stare, and their coats began to shine.

When at last they climbed blue mountain, Tuk's band came solemnly to greet them. Dall stopped and bowed a low stretch to Kenir as she approached.

Kenir also bowed. "Matriarch of blue mountain," she said to Dall.

"Fellow matriarch," Dall answered.

Kenir did not protest. Together they walked the broad, muscled back of the mountain.

"Your mountain is beautiful, Tuk," Balus said, "and it will make us great again."

"You have this almost right, Balus," Tuk said. "It is beautiful, and it will see our herd become great again. But it is not my mountain. It is ours. Yours and mine and all the herd's."

END

Kenir and Tragus lived long enough to see the herd grow and multiply and become great again.

One day not many years later, a strong young ewe, with the encouragement and advice of Dall, led a break-off band to a neighboring mountain to the west. It, too, had meadows and cliffs for the lambing and rock cavities for shelter. Tuk and the other rams visited both herds, and the new herd thrived and one day produced yet another herd. The mountains unfolding endlessly on the western horizon seemed to wait patiently for the next.

Tuk and Rim and Ovis journeyed far and found other valleys, great mountains, vast meadows, and an abundance of mineral licks. They journeyed without fear of man or wind or snow—lords of the mountain. Sometimes they wandered alone, but mostly they stayed together.

On one occasion when Ovis traveled alone, he met with a wolf pack coming from the north. He was able to lead the pack away from blue mountain and eventually escape, but he returned to the old herd so wounded he did not survive the winter.

After that, Rim and Tuk wandered longer and farther. Often Tuk forgot Ovis was gone and talked to him as they laid down game trails for new generations.

One late summer, years later, when Tuk's and Rim's horns had become heavy and battered and broken at the tips, Tuk woke to find that Rim had died in his sleep in the night. Tuk stayed a day and a night by his friend, the wind screaming without interruption over the peaks and bellowing down into the valley. Finally he turned into the wind toward the old herd on blue mountain.

After a long journey he arrived in the evening and stood at the ridge over blue mountain. He could see many lambs playing, scampering up the rock tumble to see who could get the highest, racing across the meadow, leaping and running.

The yearlings and some of the younger rams looked up to see him standing on the ridge and bowed their deepest low-stretch bows. Tuk saw that the herd would always be, and that he had been part of the always.

From the meadow below, Dall looked up at Tuk. She was old and barren, but she was still the matriarch of the herd. She knew he would not return without Rim unless Rim was dead, and she hung her head in sorrow.

Tuk sensed someone behind him and turned his head to see an enormous ram, even bigger than himself.

"Fight me, Tuk, king of blue mountain and all the mountains that it birthed," said the ram.

"My fighting days are over," Tuk said, returning his gaze to Dall.

"Fight me," the ram said again in a commanding voice. "I have heard stories that say you win every battle. I have come to prove the stories wrong."

"All stories have some truth in them," Tuk said, turning to face this bold ram.

He looked then at the giant of a ram, and, bowing his deepest low stretch, he said, "My Lord Denu."

Tuk laughed, feeling suddenly young and strong, and assumed a threat stance. Denu also presented, and they charged.

Their horns clashing sounded like far-off lightning. Threat stance, clash!, over and over until they both panted with exhaustion.

"You cannot beat me," Tuk said, though he thought that if Denu charged him one more time, he would.

"You are a true bighorn," Denu said, bowing to Tuk. "Come with me. I have a new mountain for you to see. It is glorious—even more so than your blue mountain."

Dall was staring up at Tuk, rigid, and she seemed to be trying to say something.

Tuk nodded to her, and then, with all his stories inside him, followed Lord Denu into the deep light of the evening.

Down in the meadow, the lambs pestered Dall for a story. For a long time she would not speak, but at last she began: "Tuk was born in the snow and wind of early spring. He was the biggest lamb born on the lambing cliffs that season, and for seasons out of memory . . ."

When the story was over, the lambs played, and the mountain—the mountain laughed.

James Webster

AUTHOR'S NOTE

My father, James Webster, was raised on a ranch in southern Alberta, cheek by jowl with Glacier National Park. When he was twelve years old he was already riding his horse far and wide in the foothills, exploring the lakes and rivers, coulees and forests. He loved nature and the animal world.

As an adult, he would pack his gear and hike into the Rocky Mountains in Jasper National Park, Banff National Park, Glacier National Park, and the mountains near his home in British Columbia. He walked every trail, and made a few of his own. He knew the wildlife, the names of the trees, and the names and origins of the rivers. He could read the ancient geological story in a rock wall. At one point he became intrigued with the Rocky Mountain bighorn sheep and made a study of their ranges, habitat, herd structure, and social order. For many years he trekked into wild places and photographed them and recorded his observations. He loved their independence and their ability to live in the most forbidding places. He loved their wildness. Long before it was in style, he was concerned with wilderness environments and the effects of man's encroachment.

He showed me an account he had written of a bighorn sheep through four seasons of the year. I was transported to the mountain and the simple but adaptive life of these remarkable animals. One day my father gave me a gift of all his notes.

I accepted his gift with gratitude and based this story on it. My story became a very different thing than his beautiful and perfectly accurate rendering, but we tell the stories we can. I found the entrance into my story when I read that sometimes a herd, when faced with serious range depletion, will make a migration into unknown territory.

I am grateful to my father, who taught his children to have a reverence for the beauties of the planet and all the forms of life that grace it.

—M.L.

James Webster

"Few sights are more gratifying than a herd of bighorn grazing peacefully along a mountain slope, or more stirring than that of an adult ram, horns at full curl, head held high against the backdrop of an alpine setting. It is well past the time for the wildlife and wilderness areas remaining on this continent to be regarded as a sacred trust. Each time man allows another wildlife species to fade from the face of the earth, another shadow is cast over his own quality of existence."

—James Webster, from his backcountry notes, circa 1980